# LEAD: Empowering Adaptive Leadership

**By: Antonio Wyche, LCSW & Rebecca Fernandez, LCSW**

# *Table of Contents*

# *Preface*

Leadership is a path filled with unexpected lessons that teach us adaptability, humility, and the value of growing in tandem with those we guide. It's not about authority or having all the answers—it's about learning and evolving together through every triumph and challenge. For both of us, these lessons came through real-life experiences: moments of triumph, setbacks, and the invaluable relationships we built along the way.

The idea for this book grew out of countless conversations we've had about leadership—not just what it means in theory but what it looks like in practice. Through our work with teams, organizations, and individuals, we've seen firsthand how leaders struggle to balance vision and flexibility, connection, and accountability. We realized there's a need for a clear, actionable framework to help leaders develop themselves and those they work with.

LEAD: Empowering Adaptive Leadership is our answer to that need. It's not just a manual—it's a guide born out of years of learning, trial and error, and collaboration. We wrote this book because we believe leadership can be better. We believe it's possible to build organizations that empower, not just manage; inspire, not just instruct.

For us, this isn't just professional—it's personal. We've seen how transformational leadership can change not only organizations but the lives of the people within them. That's why we're sharing this framework with you. We want to help leaders at every level grow, inspire their teams, and make a lasting impact.

As you work through this book, we hope you'll feel like you're in conversation with us—two people who've been where you are, navigating the challenges and opportunities of leadership. More than anything, we hope this guide empowers you to grow in your role and helps you create the kind of environment where others can thrive.

Thank you for letting us be part of your leadership journey. Let's strive for better leadership together.

Sincerely,

Antonio Wyche & Rebecca Fernandez

# *Introduction*

In the modern workplace, successful leadership requires a new approach. The challenges leaders face today—shifting team dynamics, diverse workforce expectations, and fast-evolving industries—call for flexibility, empathy, and decisive action. Traditional top-down, command-and-control leadership styles are proving less effective in these complex environments. Instead, leaders need to cultivate adaptability and focus on interpersonal skills that encourage collaboration and resilience.

This is where LEAD comes in.

The LEAD framework—Listening, Empathy, Accountability, and Decisiveness—offers a dynamic, actionable blueprint for responsive leadership. Each principle serves as a cornerstone, empowering leaders to cultivate trust, inspire collaboration, and adapt to their team's evolving needs. Grounded in extensive research and practice, LEAD prioritizes emotional intelligence, strategic clarity, and a people-first approach.

The foundation of the LEAD model lies in its adaptability. Each principle addresses a critical aspect of human-centered leadership, equipping leaders to engage their teams more meaningfully. Leaders who implement LEAD don't just manage tasks—they foster a supportive and motivated team culture, empowering individuals to grow and perform at their best.

In the following chapters, we will explore the LEAD principles in depth, unpack adaptive leadership styles, and examine how each element works in diverse, real-world contexts. With insights, exercises, and case studies, you will gain actionable tools to apply LEAD in your daily leadership practices.

By mastering LEAD, you will foster a team environment that is resilient, high-performing, and capable of navigating the complexities of today's workplace.

# *Chapter 1:*

# Introduction to LEAD and Adaptive Leadership

Effective leadership in today's world demands more than technical skills and business acumen—it requires a deep understanding of human behavior and adaptability. As work environments grow more dynamic and diverse, leaders need to engage with their teams in ways that inspire trust, collaboration, and loyalty. The rigid, one-size-fits-all approach to management has given way to adaptive leadership, a model that allows leaders to respond to their team members' unique needs and the shifting demands of the business landscape.

**LEAD** is a framework designed specifically for this adaptive leadership approach. It enables leaders to grow alongside their teams, creating a resilient, empowered culture capable of weathering challenges and seizing opportunities. LEAD emphasizes four core principles—Listening, Empathy, Accountability, and Decisiveness—that provide leaders with a guide for fostering sustainable, high-performance teams.

## *The Purpose of Adaptive Leadership*

The concept of adaptive leadership emerged as a response to increasingly unpredictable and complex environments. In the past, leaders might have managed effectively through strict control and oversight. However, in the fast-paced and diverse world we live in today, flexibility and a people-centered approach have become vital.

## Why Adaptive Leadership?

Research highlights the transformative power of adaptive leadership. Research suggests that teams under adaptable leaders experience significantly higher engagement, improved performance, and reduced turnover rates. These findings underscore adaptability's critical role in fostering dynamic, successful workplaces. Adaptive leadership doesn't abandon goals or structure; instead, it enhances leaders' ability to listen, connect, and respond to team needs as situations evolve. This approach recognizes that leadership is not a set of fixed practices but a dynamic process.

## Overview of LEAD Principles

The **LEAD** model was developed to distill essential qualities of adaptive leadership into actionable principles. Let's briefly explore each principle and its role in shaping effective leadership:

1. **Listening** - The foundation of trust and understanding, listening is an essential skill for any leader. Effective listening allows leaders to understand their team members' challenges, motivations, and perspectives. By truly listening, leaders create a supportive environment where individuals feel valued and are more likely to engage openly.

2. **Empathy** - Empathy goes beyond basic understanding; it requires leaders to recognize and

validate their team members' feelings. Empathy is especially crucial in high-stress situations, as it fosters a sense of belonging and support, helping to alleviate feelings of isolation or frustration.

3. **Accountability** - Accountability ensures that team members feel a sense of ownership over their work and are held to consistent standards. A culture of accountability promotes transparency, trust, and mutual respect. Leaders who model accountability encourage their teams to take responsibility, creating a reliable and cohesive group.

4. **Decisiveness** - Decisiveness enables leaders to provide clear direction and guidance. While adaptability is essential, teams also rely on leaders who can make informed, timely decisions. Decisive leaders instill confidence in their teams and create momentum by setting a clear course of action.

Together, these four principles create a robust framework for leaders to cultivate resilient, adaptable, and motivated teams.

# *LEAD in Action: Cross-Industry Applications*

The versatility of the LEAD model is one of its greatest strengths. It applies across industries, supporting teams in various fields, including healthcare, education, technology, and sales. Here are a few examples of how LEAD principles can make a difference in different environments:

- **Listening**: In a fast-paced hospital setting, a nurse manager may hold daily check-ins with their team, providing a safe space to voice concerns and share insights about patient care. By listening actively, the manager fosters trust, reduces burnout, and improves patient outcomes.

- **Empathy**: A school principal facing high teacher turnover might implement "empathy sessions," allowing teachers to openly discuss challenges and concerns. This practice validates teachers' experiences, leading to improved morale and retention.

- **Accountability**: A sales manager could establish weekly accountability check-ins where team members report progress on their targets. This process reinforces individual responsibility and team-wide commitment, driving performance and customer satisfaction.

- **Decisiveness**: In a tech start-up, a project leader might empower team members to make key decisions within defined parameters, promoting innovation and timely project completion. By fostering decisiveness, the leader accelerates progress and encourages independent problem-solving.

These examples illustrate how LEAD principles can be adapted to suit the unique demands of any industry.

# *Why LEAD Works Across Different Industries*

The LEAD model thrives in diverse settings because it meets universal human needs. These principles resonate deeply, fostering a workplace culture built on respect, connection, and mutual commitment. By cultivating such a positive environment, the LEAD model proves effective across industries and fields, making it a versatile framework for success.

# *Getting Started with LEAD*

As we move forward in this book, we will explore each principle of LEAD in greater depth. The chapters that follow provide:

- **Detailed Explanations**: A thorough look at each principle, its purpose, and how it can be applied in various scenarios.

- **Practical Exercises**: Activities that reinforce the principles, encouraging team growth and resilience.

- **Real-World Applications**: Anecdotes and case studies illustrating LEAD in action.

- **Challenges and Solutions**: Common obstacles leaders may face, along with strategies for overcoming them.

By the end of this book, you will have a toolkit of strategies for building a high-performing and adaptable team. Whether you are a first-time leader or a seasoned executive, LEAD provides a pathway to a culture where collaboration, accountability, and empowerment thrive.

# *Chapter 2:*

# The LEAD Principles – Listening, Empathy, Accountability, and Decisiveness

## *Introduction to LEAD Principles*

The four LEAD principles—Listening, Empathy, Accountability, and Decisiveness—are abstract concepts and practical skills that adaptive leaders can actively develop and apply. Each principle uniquely creates a supportive, results-oriented team environment where leaders and team members alike can thrive.

In this chapter, we'll explore each principle in detail, outlining why it matters, how to practice it, and examples from various industries demonstrating its impact.

## *Listening: The Foundation of Connection*

### *Why Listening Matters*

Listening is the cornerstone of effective communication and the foundation upon which trust is built. Leaders who actively listen create a culture of openness where team members feel heard, valued, and understood. Listening goes beyond simply hearing words; it requires full engagement, attention to non-verbal cues, and a genuine desire to understand the speaker's perspective.

Active listening enables leaders to make more informed decisions, build stronger relationships, and anticipate team needs before they escalate into challenges. When leaders prioritize listening, they establish a respectful environment that encourages team members to share ideas and voice concerns openly.

## *Techniques for Effective Listening*

1. **Practice Active Listening**

   o   Maintain eye contact, nod, and avoid interruptions to show you're fully engaged.

   o   Use phrases like "Tell me more about that" or "How do you see this issue?" to prompt further insights.

2. **Paraphrase and Summarize**

   o   Reflect back on what the speaker has said to confirm understanding, e.g., "So you're concerned about the deadline—do I have that right?"

   o   Paraphrasing reassures the speaker that their thoughts have been understood and allows them to clarify if needed.

3. **Eliminate Distractions**

   o   During one-on-one or team discussions, silence your phone, close your laptop, and give your undivided attention. This signals respect and helps you remain fully present.

# *Real-World Example: Listening*

In a hospital setting, a nurse manager noticed high levels of stress among her team due to increased patient loads. She decided to hold daily team huddles, where each nurse could share concerns and ideas for improving workflow. By actively listening and acknowledging her team's challenges, the manager fostered a supportive work environment that improved morale and patient care outcomes.

# *Empathy: Building Resilience and Trust*

## *The Power of Empathy in Leadership*

Empathy is connecting with and understanding others' feelings, perspectives, and experiences. Leaders who demonstrate empathy foster a supportive culture where team members feel appreciated and valued, particularly in stressful or challenging situations. Empathy strengthens resilience by providing a safe space for team members to share difficulties and receive validation, thus reducing burnout and increasing team cohesion.

## *Techniques for Empathetic Leadership*

1. **Acknowledge Emotions**

   o Recognize when team members display signs of stress or frustration. Simple acknowledgments like, "I understand this is a difficult time," can make a difference in how supported they feel.

2. **Ask Open-Ended Questions**

    o Show empathy by asking questions that allow team members to express themselves, e.g., "What do you need right now to feel supported?"

3. **Demonstrate Flexibility and Support**

    o Show that you're willing to adjust workloads or deadlines in times of high stress. This responsiveness reinforces that you value their well-being.

## *Real-World Example: Empathy*

A principal noticed a high turnover rate among her teaching staff, primarily due to burnout. She initiated "empathy sessions," where teachers were encouraged to discuss challenges without fear of judgment. The feedback allowed the principal to implement changes, like adjusting workloads and redistributing administrative tasks. This empathy-driven approach improved teacher morale and reduced turnover.

# *Accountability: The Backbone of Performance*

## *The Role of Accountability in Leadership*

Accountability is the commitment to taking responsibility for one's actions, decisions, and outcomes. Leaders who foster accountability create an environment where team members understand their roles, meet their commitments, and trust one another to deliver on their responsibilities. Accountability doesn't only involve pointing out mistakes; it encourages ownership, growth, and a higher reliability standard.

## *Techniques for Building Accountability*

1. **Set Clear Expectations**

   - Define each team member's role, responsibilities, and performance standards. Make sure everyone understands their individual and collective goals from the start.

2. **Provide Regular Feedback**

   - Review progress consistently, offering constructive feedback that promotes growth and improvement rather than focusing on faults.

3. **Encourage Peer Accountability**

   o Foster a culture where team members feel comfortable holding each other accountable through shared goals, check-ins, and collaborative problem-solving.

## *Real-World Example: Accountability*

A regional sales manager introduced weekly check-ins, where each team member reported on their progress toward targets. This process reinforced individual accountability and promoted a strong sense of teamwork and commitment. Over time, the practice led to improved sales performance and strengthened the team's cohesion.

# *Decisiveness: Empowering Team Autonomy*

## *The Importance of Decisiveness in Leadership*

Decisiveness is the ability to make informed, confident decisions quickly and effectively. Leaders who are decisive provide clarity, momentum, and direction, empowering their teams to act independently and confidently. Decisiveness is not about making hasty choices; it's about weighing available information, choosing a course of action, and moving forward without hesitation.

## *Techniques for Decisive Leadership*

1. **Make Timely Decisions**

   o   Avoid "analysis paralysis" by setting reasonable deadlines for decision-making. Commit to a choice based on the best data available at the time.

2. **Delegate Decision-Making**

   o   Encourage team members to make decisions within their areas of expertise. This not only speeds up processes but also builds trust and autonomy.

3. **Embrace Calculated Risks**

   o   Foster a culture where mistakes are seen as learning opportunities. Encouraging risk-taking can help teams innovate and adapt more rapidly.

## *Real-World Example: Decisiveness*

A tech project manager faced multiple delays on a critical software project. After assessing the situation, she reassigned tasks and streamlined communication channels to ensure smoother collaboration. Her clear, decisive actions allowed the team to refocus and meet project deadlines. This decision-making approach fostered greater autonomy and empowered team members to take ownership of their roles.

# *Conclusion: Integrating LEAD Principles into Leadership Practice*

The principles of Listening, Empathy, Accountability, and Decisiveness are not just individual skills; they are interdependent and mutually reinforcing. Leaders who actively practice these principles build resilient, collaborative, and adaptable teams. The more consistently these principles are applied, the more they create a culture of trust, openness, and high performance.

As we move forward in this book, we will explore how these principles can be tailored to individual team members' needs through adaptive leadership styles. By applying these practices thoughtfully and consistently, leaders can empower their teams to reach their full potential.

# *Chapter 3:*

# Adapting Leadership Styles with LEAD Principles

## *Introduction to Adaptive Leadership Styles*

One of the hallmarks of effective leadership is the ability to adapt to the unique needs, skill levels, and development stages of team members. Rather than applying a uniform style to everyone, leaders who are adaptable can meet individuals where they are, providing the right balance of guidance, support, structure, and autonomy. The **LEAD framework** allows leaders to tailor their approach through four adaptive leadership styles:

1. **Guiding** (Listening-focused)

2. **Supporting** (Empathy-focused)

3. **Challenging** (Accountability-focused)

4. **Empowering** (Decisiveness-focused)

Each style is specifically aligned with one of the LEAD principles, helping leaders respond effectively to different team members' needs.

# *Guiding Leadership Style: Listening-Focused*

## *Purpose*

The Guiding style is ideal for team members who are new, inexperienced, or uncertain in their roles. These individuals often need clear direction and frequent feedback to build confidence and understand expectations. Listening is the primary LEAD principle in this style, helping leaders discern each team member's needs, challenges, and motivations.

## *When to Use the Guiding Style*

The Guiding style is most effective when team members:

- Are new to the organization or role.

- Lack of familiarity with tasks, processes, or expectations.

- Require detailed instructions and close supervision to feel comfortable and competent.

## *Leader's Role in the Guiding Style*

In the Guiding style, the leader's role includes:

- **Active Listening**: Create an open environment by listening attentively to team members' questions, concerns, and feedback.

- **Clear Instruction**: Provide detailed, step-by-step guidance to ensure understanding.

- **Encouraging Questions**: Reinforce clarity by welcoming questions and promoting an open dialogue.

## *Example Actions for the Guiding Style*

1. **One-on-One Meetings**: Schedule regular check-ins to discuss goals, answer questions, and provide feedback on progress.

2. **Detailed Task Instructions**: Break down tasks into manageable steps and confirm understanding before proceeding.

3. **Active Listening**: During meetings, actively listen and show that team members' perspectives are valued.

## *Case Example: Guiding*

A junior analyst, Alex, recently joined a data analysis team. Lacking experience, she felt uncertain in her role. Her manager, Rachel, adopted the Guiding style, meeting weekly with Alex to review assignments and provide step-by-step instructions on software tools. By listening to Alex's concerns and offering clear guidance, Rachel helped her build confidence and develop her skills more effectively.

# *Supporting Leadership Style: Empathy-Focused*

## *Purpose*

The Supporting style is designed for team members who have some experience but may lack confidence or face challenges in their roles. Here, **Empathy** is the core LEAD principle, as leaders focus on providing emotional support, encouragement, and constructive feedback to help team members build confidence and overcome obstacles.

## *When to Use the Supporting Style*

The Supporting style is most effective for team members who:

- Have some experience but feel unsure or overwhelmed.
- Need encouragement to build confidence and motivation.
- Benefit from empathy and support to navigate challenges.

## *Leader's Role in the Supporting Style*

In the Supporting style, the leader's role includes:

- **Showing Empathy**: Validate team members' emotions, especially in stressful situations.

- **Positive Reinforcement**: Recognize achievements, even small ones, to boost morale.

- **Constructive Feedback**: Offer feedback that emphasizes strengths and growth opportunities.

## *Example Actions for the Supporting Style*

1. **Acknowledging Efforts**: Celebrate contributions, especially during challenging times, to reinforce resilience.

2. **Validating Concerns**: Listen empathetically to team members' challenges and offer guidance or flexibility as needed.

3. **Encouragement for Growth**: Encourage team members to take on new responsibilities to help them gain confidence.

## *Case Example: Supporting*

John, a first-year teacher, often felt overwhelmed by classroom management. His principal, Melissa, used a Supporting approach by meeting with him bi-weekly to discuss his progress, validate his efforts, and provide constructive feedback. Melissa's empathy and encouragement helped John build confidence, allowing him to handle classroom challenges more effectively.

# *Challenging Leadership Style: Accountability-Focused*

## *Purpose*

The Challenging style is designed for team members who are capable but need more structure and accountability to reach their full potential. **Accountability** is the primary LEAD principle here, reinforcing responsibility, commitment, and a higher standard of performance. This style helps team members consistently align with goals, meet expectations, and contribute.

## *When to Use the Challenging Style*

The Challenging style is effective for team members who:

- Are competent in their roles but need consistency or follow-through.

- Require accountability and feedback to maintain or improve performance.

- Benefit from clear goals and structured expectations.

## *Leader's Role in the Challenging Style*

In the Challenging style, the leader's role includes:

- **Setting Clear Expectations**: Define specific goals, deadlines, and performance standards.

- **Providing Regular Feedback**: Offer constructive feedback to keep team members aligned with objectives.

- **Encouraging Peer Accountability**: Cultivate a culture where team members support each other's progress.

## *Example Actions for the Challenging Style*

1. **Goal-Setting Meetings**: Collaborate with team members to set measurable goals and hold regular check-ins to track progress.

2. **Consistent Feedback**: Provide timely, constructive feedback on achievements and areas for improvement.

3. **Peer Review Systems**: Encourage team members to hold each other accountable by sharing updates on shared goals.

## *Case Example: Challenging*

Sophia, a skilled designer, frequently struggled to meet deadlines. Her manager, Peter, adopted a Challenging approach, setting clear project timelines and implementing a peer review process. By holding Sophia accountable and reinforcing deadlines, Peter helped her develop better time management, ultimately improving her reliability and performance.

# *Empowering Leadership Style: Decisiveness-Focused*

## *Purpose*

The Empowering style is ideal for team members who are highly skilled, confident, and ready to take on greater responsibility. In this style, **Decisiveness** is the primary LEAD principle, as leaders encourage independent decision-making, autonomy, and ownership over work. This style empowers experienced team members to take the lead and grow in their roles.

## *When to Use the Empowering Style*

The Empowering style is best suited for team members who:

- Are experienced, motivated, and consistent in meeting performance expectations.

- Are ready to make independent decisions and take ownership of their roles.

- Thrive in environments that allow autonomy and trust.

## *Leader's Role in the Empowering Style*

In the Empowering style, the leader's role includes:

- **Delegating Authority**: Trust team members to make decisions within their roles.

- **Encouraging Risk-Taking**: Support team members in exploring innovative solutions and taking calculated risks.

- **Being Available as an Advisor**: Offer guidance when needed but avoid micromanaging daily tasks.

## *Example Actions for the Empowering Style*

1. **Decision-Making Authority**: Allow team members to lead projects or initiatives, giving them full control over decisions.

2. **Risk-Taking Encouragement**: Empower team members to try new ideas, framing mistakes as opportunities to learn.

3. **Strategic Check-Ins**: Periodically check in to discuss progress and offer input without overseeing daily tasks.

## *Case Example: Empowering*

Jessica, a senior marketing strategist, consistently met and exceeded her goals. Her manager, Tom, adopted the Empowering approach, allowing Jessica to lead major campaigns independently. Tom's trust and autonomy led to Jessica's innovative campaigns and increased job satisfaction, as she felt a strong sense of ownership and autonomy in her role.

# LEAD Adaptive Leadership Styles Matrix

The following matrix summarizes the four adaptive leadership styles within the LEAD framework. This matrix serves as a quick reference for determining the appropriate style based on each team member's needs:

| Leadership Style | Primary LEAD Principle | When to Use | Leader's Role |
|---|---|---|---|
| **Guiding** | Listening | New or uncertain team members | Active listening, clear instructions, encourage questions |
| **Supporting** | Empathy | Moderately skilled team members needing confidence | Show empathy, positive reinforcement, constructive feedback |
| **Challenging** | Accountability | Skilled team members needing consistency | Set expectations, provide regular feedback, encourage peer accountability |
| **Empowering** | Decisiveness | Experienced team members ready for autonomy | Delegate authority, encourage risk-taking, act as an advisor |

# *Conclusion: Adapting Leadership for Individual Growth*

By applying these four adaptive styles, leaders can provide the right balance of guidance, support, accountability, and autonomy to meet each team member's development needs. This approach fosters a team culture where individuals feel valued, empowered, and capable of contributing effectively to shared goals. Leaders who use the LEAD framework to adapt their approach create an environment where both the team and the organization can thrive.

# *Chapter 4:*

# LEAD Synergy

## *Introduction to LEAD Synergy*

**LEAD Synergy** is a structured framework designed to guide leaders through each phase of building a resilient, empowered team. This pathway consists of four key stages, each aligned with one of the LEAD principles:

1. **Connecting** (Listening) – Building trust and open communication.

2. **Strengthening** (Empathy) – Creating resilience as the team faces challenges.

3. **Aligning** (Accountability) – Reinforcing commitment and accountability toward shared goals.

4. **Empowering** (Decisiveness) – Enabling team members to operate with independence and confidence.

Each stage builds on the last, supporting leaders as they move from hands-on involvement to a more advisory role, empowering team members to take ownership of their work. Leaders who understand and apply each stage of the LEAD pathway are better equipped to create an adaptable, high-performance team.

# Stage 1: Connecting – Building a Foundation with Listening

## Overview

The Connecting stage is the foundation of team development, focusing on establishing relationships, building trust, and creating open lines of communication. **Listening** is the guiding principle in this stage, as it enables leaders to understand their team members' strengths, motivations, and concerns. Effective listening fosters a positive, collaborative team culture and sets the tone for productive engagement.

## When to Use the Connecting Stage

The Connecting stage is especially valuable for:

- Newly formed teams or teams with recent new members.

- Teams experiencing a significant change, such as restructuring or shifts in responsibilities.

- Teams with low morale or trust issues

## Leader's Role in the Connecting Stage

In this stage, the leader acts as a facilitator, focusing on setting the groundwork for open communication. Key responsibilities include:

- **One-on-One Introductions**: Meet with each team member individually to understand their goals, strengths, and potential challenges.

- **Team Building Activities**: Facilitate activities that allow team members to share personal cr professional experiences.

- **Establishing Communication Norms**: Set clear expectations for respectful communicatior, active listening, and openness.

## *Example Actions for the Connecting Stage*

1. **One-on-One Meetings**: Meet individually with each team member, asking questions like "What are your goals?" and "How can I support you in this role?"

2. **Team Introduction Session**: Conduct a session where each member introduces themselves and shares something unique about their background or interests.

3. **Set Clear Norms**: Outline and reinforce norms for team discussions, including respect, listening, and constructive feedback.

## *Case Example: Connecting*

Andrea, a new manager at a local non-profit, prioritized the Connecting stage when she took over her team. She held individual meetings to learn each team member's career goals, previous experiences, and support needs. By fostering open dialogue, Andrea established trust, which helped the team transition smoothly and laid the foundation for collaboration.

### *Common Challenges and Solutions*

- **Challenge**: Team members may feel hesitant to open up initially.

  - o **Solution**: Create a safe space by listening actively, showing genuine interest, and validating their input.

- **Challenge**: Some team members may dominate discussions while others stay quiet.

  - o **Solution**: Encourage balanced participation by directly inviting quieter members to share their perspectives.

# *Stage 2: Strengthening – Building Resilience with Empathy*

## *Overview*

The Strengthening stage is essential for building resilience within the team as it begins to face challenges, such as high workloads, conflicts, or external pressures. **Empathy** is the guiding principle in this stage, as it enables leaders to support their team members emotionally and mentally, helping them navigate stress and stay engaged.

## *When to Use the Strengthening Stage*

The Strengthening stage is particularly useful when:

- Teams are under high stress due to demanding projects or tight deadlines.

- Conflicts or misunderstandings are affecting team dynamics.

- Team members display signs of burnout or disengagement.

## *Leader's Role in the Strengthening Stage*

In this stage, the leader acts as a coach, focusing on providing emotional support. Key responsibilities include:

- **Empathy Check-Ins**: Hold regular one-on-one check-ins to understand team members' stress levels and well-being.

- **Conflict Resolution Facilitation**: Encourage open discussions when conflicts arise, using empathy-driven strategies to foster understanding.

- **Positive Reinforcement**: Recognize efforts and achievements, especially when team members handle challenges well.

## *Example Actions for the Strengthening Stage*

1. **Empathy Check-Ins**: Schedule regular one-on-one meetings to ask about team members' workloads and provide support as needed.

2. **Facilitate Open Dialogue**: When conflicts arise, encourage team members to openly share their perspectives in a respectful environment.

3. **Reinforce Positives**: Recognize and celebrate resilience, highlighting individuals who navigate challenges effectively.

## *Case Example: Strengthening*

Jason, a team lead at a healthcare facility, noticed his team was feeling overwhelmed by increased patient loads and new safety protocols. During weekly check-ins, he validated their concerns and offered words of encouragement, helping to reduce stress and foster resilience.

## *Common Challenges and Solutions*

- **Challenge**: Team members may feel stressed by increased workloads.

    o **Solution**: Acknowledge their struggles and, if possible, provide additional resources or adjust deadlines.

- **Challenge**: Conflicts or misunderstandings may arise under pressure.

    o **Solution**: Facilitate empathy-driven conflict resolution, encouraging team members to listen to each other's perspectives.

# *Stage 3: Aligning – Fostering Accountability and Commitment*

## *Overview*

The Aligning stage focuses on reinforcing accountability and commitment to shared goals as team members become more cohesive and aligned in their roles. **Accountability** is the primary LEAD principle at this stage, as it ensures that each member takes ownership of their work and understands the importance of meeting expectations.

## *When to Use the Aligning Stage*

The Aligning stage is appropriate for teams that:

- Are gaining experience and cohesion but need clarity on goals.

- Benefit from defined expectations to keep performance consistent.

- Require reinforcement of shared responsibilities to achieve collective goals.

## *Leader's Role in the Aligning Stage*

In this stage, the leader acts as a manager, reinforcing standards and holding team members accountable. Key responsibilities include:

- **Goal Setting and Accountability Meetings**: Collaboratively set measurable goals and hold regular check-ins to discuss progress.

- **Encouraging Peer Accountability**: Foster a culture where team members feel responsible for each other's success.

- **Providing Structured Feedback**: Offer regular feedback to reinforce accountability and recognize achievements.

## *Example Actions for the Aligning Stage*

1. **Goal-Setting Sessions**: Collaborate with team members to set specific, measurable goals that align with team objectives.

2. **Accountability Meetings**: Schedule weekly or bi-weekly meetings where team members report on progress and share challenges.

3. **Peer Accountability Practices**: Encourage team members to support each other in meeting objectives.

## *Case Example: Aligning*

Lily, a senior manager, introduced weekly accountability meetings for her product development team. Each member reported on their progress, which fostered transparency, trust, and a shared commitment to project goals.

### *Common Challenges and Solutions*

- **Challenge**: Some team members may struggle to meet expectations.

  - **Solution**: Offer constructive feedback and support improvement through targeted coaching.

- **Challenge**: Peer accountability may feel uncomfortable for some.

  - **Solution**: Normalize constructive feedback by modeling respectful and constructive feedback during meetings.

# Stage 4: Empowering – Enabling Autonomy with Decisiveness

### *Overview*

In the Empowering stage, the team is ready to operate independently, with each member confidently handling their responsibilities. **Decisiveness** is the guiding principle, as leaders empower team members to make decisions, take calculated risks, and take ownership of their roles.

### *When to Use the Empowering Stage*

The Empowering stage is suited for teams that:

- Have consistently demonstrated high performance and commitment.

- Are prepared to make independent decisions aligned with organizational goals.

- Thrive in an environment of trust and autonomy.

## *Leader's Role in the Empowering Stage*

In this stage, the leader acts as an advisor, providing guidance when needed but allowing team members to make decisions independently. Key responsibilities include:

- **Delegating Decision-Making**: Trust team members with authority within their roles.

- **Recognizing Initiative**: Celebrate team members' independent actions and achievements.

- **Strategic Check-Ins**: Schedule occasional check-ins to ensure alignment with broader goals without micromanaging.

## *Example Actions for the Empowering Stage*

1. **Delegated Authority**: Allow team members to lead projects and make decisions within their scope of work.

2. **Risk-Taking Support**: Encourage experimentation, framing mistakes as opportunities to learn.

3. **High-Level Check-Ins**: Hold strategic check-ins to discuss overall progress and provide guidance as needed.

## *Case Example: Empowering*

Liam, a director at a software company, observed that his team was highly capable and independent. He gradually delegated more project responsibilities to team leads, empowering them to decide on resource allocation and timelines, boosting morale and efficiency.

## *Common Challenges and Solutions*

- **Challenge**: Some team members may seek approval for minor decisions.

    - **Solution**: Reinforce autonomy by encouraging team members to trust their judgment and make decisions independently. Provide reassurance that mistakes are part of growth and learning.

- **Challenge**: Risk of inconsistency in quality or standards.

    - **Solution**: Set clear benchmarks for quality and offer guidelines for maintaining standards. Provide guidance on critical decisions to ensure alignment with organizational goals.

# *Conclusion of LEAD Synergy*

LEAD Synergy offers a structured, progressive approach to building a resilient, empowered team. By moving through each stage—Connecting, Strengthening, Aligning, and Empowering—leaders can adapt their approach as team members grow. This process fosters trust, accountability, and independent decision-making, creating a team that is prepared to take ownership of their roles and contribute effectively to organizational goals.

Leaders who apply the LEAD Synergy model transition from hands-on guidance to a supportive advisory role, allowing their teams to function autonomously. By focusing on the appropriate LEAD principle at each stage, leaders cultivate an environment where team members feel seen, valued, and capable, contributing to high performance and sustainable success.

In the next chapter, **Chapter 5: Challenges in Implementing LEAD and Solutions**, we'll address common obstacles leaders face when applying the LEAD framework. We'll explore strategies for overcoming resistance to change, balancing empathy and accountability, and sustaining LEAD principles over time.

# *Chapter 5:*

# Challenges in Implementing LEAD and Solutions

## *Introduction*

Implementing **LEAD Synergy** can transform a team's culture and performance but requires leaders to navigate challenges skillfully. While the LEAD framework is straightforward, the process of incorporating **Listening, Empathy, Accountability, and Decisiveness** can involve overcoming initial resistance, balancing sometimes opposing principles, and sustaining new habits over time.

This chapter will address five key challenges and offer practical solutions for each:

1. **Resistance to Change**

2. **Balancing Empathy and Accountability**

3. **Developing Peer Accountability**

4. **Empowering Autonomy without Losing Control**

5. **Sustaining LEAD Principles Over Time**

By proactively addressing these challenges, leaders can embed LEAD principles as a natural part of their team's culture, creating a lasting foundation for resilience, trust, and high performance.

# *Challenge 1: Resistance to Change*

## *Overview*

Resistance to change is a common hurdle when introducing any new framework. Team members may feel hesitant about new communication norms, accountability structures, or evolving expectations from their leader. Adjusting to LEAD often involves shifting established mindsets and habits, which can create uncertainty.

## *Solution*

1. **Communicate the Vision**

   o Explain the purpose of LEAD Synergy and its benefits for the team. When team members understand how LEAD will improve collaboration, productivity, and trust, they are more likely to embrace the transition. Share success stories from other teams or organizations to illustrate the impact of LEAD.

2. **Start Gradually**

   o Introduce LEAD principles one stage at a time. Begin with the **Connecting stage** by focusing on listening and open communication. Allow time for team members to adjust before moving to the next stage, gradually building confidence and buy-in.

3. **Seek Feedback**

- o Regularly ask for feedback from team members about their experiences with the LEAD approach. By addressing concerns and adjusting the pace of implementation based on feedback, leaders show that they respect and value team members' comfort and input.

## *Example*

Carlos, a retail manager, faced initial pushback when introducing LEAD principles. Team members were skeptical about structured accountability and open communication. By clearly explaining LEAD's benefits and starting with a focus on listening, Carlos slowly built trust and engaged his team in the new approach.

# *Challenge 2: Balancing Empathy and Accountability*

## *Overview*

One of the most common challenges leaders face is balancing empathy and accountability. Focusing too heavily on empathy may lead to relaxed standards while overemphasizing accountability can erode morale and trust. Effective leaders must find a middle ground where team members feel both supported and responsible.

## *Solution*

1. **Set Clear Expectations from the Start**

   o   Begin with well-defined roles, responsibilities, and goals. Clarity provides a foundation for accountability and helps team members understand that empathy doesn't mean a lack of structure or expectations.

2. **Lead with Empathy, Follow with Accountability**

   o   When team members face challenges, start by showing empathy—acknowledge their experiences and offer support. Then, clearly outline steps for improvement or solutions. For example, if a team member is struggling with deadlines, provide initial support and follow up with an improvement plan that reinforces accountability.

3. **Model Both Values**

   o   Demonstrate that it's possible to balance empathy with high standards. Acknowledge challenges, validate emotions, and reinforce the importance of meeting goals. When team members see that their leader can embody both values, they are more likely to follow suit.

## *Example*

Laura, a nonprofit director, noticed her team struggled to meet deadlines. She responded by showing empathy, listening to each team member's challenges, and providing support. However, she also emphasized the importance of accountability, outlining clear expectations. This approach improved both morale and performance, as her team felt understood yet motivated to meet their responsibilities.

# *Challenge 3: Developing Peer Accountability*

## *Overview*

Creating a culture of **peer accountability** can be challenging, as team members may feel uncomfortable providing feedback to their colleagues. For peer accountability to succeed, team members need to understand that constructive feedback is beneficial, not personal and that it can foster trust and collaboration when applied thoughtfully.

## *Solution*

1. **Normalize Constructive Feedback**

    o  Encourage open feedback by modeling it yourself. Praise team members who give constructive feedback to peers, making it a valued part of the team culture. When leaders embrace feedback as a positive tool for growth, team members are more likely to follow.

2. **Introduce Structured Peer Review**

   o Implement a structured peer review system where team members can assess each other's work or provide feedback in a supportive, non-judgmental format. Structured peer reviews make accountability a natural part of the process, helping team members become comfortable with it.

3. **Provide Feedback Training**

   o Offer training on how to give and receive feedback effectively. Teach team members to focus on specific behaviors and outcomes rather than personal characteristics, which builds a respectful and constructive feedback culture.

## *Example*

David, a program director at a consulting firm, wanted his team to adopt peer accountability to improve project efficiency. He introduced weekly check-ins where each team member shared goals and progress. This consistent practice fostered an environment where feedback was expected, making team members more comfortable supporting each other's progress.

# *Challenge 4: Empowering Autonomy without Losing Control*

## *Overview*

In the **Empowering stage**, leaders may find it challenging to balance team autonomy with maintaining quality and standards. While leaders need to step back to foster independence, autonomy can lead to inconsistency if team members make decisions without alignment on expectations.

## *Solution*

1. **Set Clear Boundaries and Standards**

   o Define clear parameters for decision-making and establish quality benchmarks. Let team members know when they have the authority to make independent choices and when it's important to consult you or the team.

2. **Emphasize Ownership and Consequences**

   o Help team members understand that autonomy comes with responsibility. Celebrate their successes, but also encourage them to learn from their mistakes. Reinforce that they are accountable for their choices and outcomes.

3. **Periodic Strategic Check-Ins**

   o Schedule occasional check-ins to review progress and discuss challenges. This approach maintains alignment with broader goals while avoiding micromanagement, allowing team members to operate independently.

## *Example*

Emma, a local resource center director, empowered her experienced team by granting them autonomy in daily decision-making. She balanced trust with oversight by setting quarterly check-ins to discuss strategic alignment and standards. Her team responded with increased confidence and innovation, knowing they had both independence and support.

# *Challenge 5: Sustaining LEAD Principles Over Time*

## *Overview*

Implementing LEAD principles is one thing; sustaining them over time requires consistent reinforcement. Without ongoing commitment, teams may revert to previous habits, and the impact of LEAD can diminish. Leaders must actively integrate LEAD principles into their everyday practices to make them a lasting part of team culture.

## *Solution*

1. **Reinforce LEAD Principles Regularly**

   o Begin team meetings with a brief review of one LEAD principle or highlight recent examples of team members who embody these values. Regular discussions keep LEAD top-of-mind and reinforce its importance.

2. **Celebrate Milestones and Progress**

   o Acknowledge and celebrate the team's progress as they advance through the stages of LEAD. Celebrating achievements reinforces commitment to the pathway and motivates the team to continue applying LEAD principles.

3. **Provide Ongoing Development Opportunities**

   o Offer training, workshops, or mentorship programs aligned with LEAD principles. Continuous learning and development help sustain the impact of LEAD by encouraging team members to grow their skills and internalize these values.

## *Example*

Lydia, a manager of team leads in an educational organization, noticed her team slipping back into old habits a few months after implementing LEAD. To sustain progress, she began each meeting with a brief discussion of a LEAD principle and recognized team members who applied it effectively. This consistent reinforcement helped embed LEAD principles into her team's everyday practices.

## *Conclusion: Overcoming Challenges for Long-Term Success*

Implementing LEAD Synergy requires intentionality, flexibility, and patience. By anticipating obstacles such as resistance to change, balancing empathy with accountability, and managing team autonomy, leaders can apply proactive strategies to embed LEAD as a lasting part of team culture.

By overcoming these challenges, leaders foster a team that values listening, empathy, accountability, and decisiveness, and they create an adaptable, high-performance culture that evolves alongside the team's needs. As we continue, **Chapter 6: The Role of Communication in Adaptive Leadership** will discuss how open, effective communication underpins LEAD principles and enables adaptive leaders to successfully guide their teams through each stage.

# *Chapter 6:*

# The Role of Communication in Adaptive Leadership

## *Introduction*

In any leadership framework, communication is the bridge between ideas and action, yet it becomes even more critical in adaptive leadership. Adaptive leaders need to connect with their team members on a personal level, anticipate and address their concerns, and provide clarity amid uncertainty. Communication is the thread that binds each of the **LEAD** principles—**Listening, Empathy, Accountability,** and **Decisiveness**—into an effective, adaptable leadership approach.

This chapter explores how adaptive leaders can use communication to implement LEAD principles, discussing essential communication skills, strategies for fostering transparency, and real-world applications for building a culture that encourages open dialogue.

# *Listening and Communication: Building Trust and Openness*

## *Why Communication Matters for Listening*

Listening as a principle in LEAD requires more than just absorbing information—it involves creating an atmosphere where team members feel safe to share their perspectives and ideas. When leaders actively communicate their willingness to listen, it reassures team members that their voices matter, fostering trust and openness.

## *Techniques for Effective Communication in Listening*

1. **Ask Open-Ended Questions**

   o Use questions like "What challenges are you facing?" or "How can I support you better?" to open the door to meaningful dialogue.

2. **Acknowledge Contributions**

   o When team members share insights, acknowledge their input to show you're actively listening. Statements like, "I appreciate you sharing that" or "That's an important point" reinforce the value of their perspectives.

3. **Encourage Two-Way Feedback**

   o Regularly ask for feedback on your communication style and leadership approach. By showing that you're open to feedback, you model the listening-focused behavior you wish to see in your team.

## *Real-World Example: Creating a Culture of Openness in a Call Center*

In a high-stress call center environment, a team leader noticed that employees often hesitated to share their concerns. The leader fostered a more open environment by establishing a weekly "listening session" where team members could share feedback on processes. This proactive listening led to improved workflows and increased job satisfaction.

# *Empathy and Communication: Creating a Safe Space for Emotional Expression*

## *The Role of Communication in Empathy*

Empathy in leadership means creating a space where team members feel comfortable expressing their emotions and challenges. Effective communication makes empathy actionable—leaders show team members that their struggles are understood and validated. Empathy-driven communication not only boosts morale but also supports team resilience.

## *Techniques for Empathy-Focused Communication*

1. **Use Validating Language**

   o Recognize team members' emotions with phrases like "I understand this is challenging" or

"It sounds like this has been difficult for you." Validating language demonstrates understanding and support.

2. **Hold Empathy Check-Ins**

   o Schedule regular one-on-one check-ins focused on understanding team members' stressors and overall well-being. By making empathy part of routine communication, leaders show they care about team members' emotional health.

3. **Respond with Flexibility**

   o When possible, offer flexible solutions in response to stressors (e.g., adjusting workloads or deadlines), demonstrating that you're receptive to their needs.

## *Real-World Example: Empathy in Retail Management*

Sarah, a retail manager, observed increased stress levels among her team due to long hours and holiday rushes. She acknowledged these challenges by holding regular empathy check-ins and offered flexible scheduling as a solution. This empathy-driven approach helped her team feel understood and supported, which improved morale and reduced turnover.

# *Accountability and Communication: Clarifying Expectations and Feedback*

## *The Importance of Communication in Accountability*

Accountability requires clear, consistent communication. Leaders must articulate expectations, provide timely feedback, and create a transparent environment where team members understand their responsibilities and the consequences of their actions. Accountability-driven communication keeps everyone aligned and fosters a sense of ownership.

## *Techniques for Accountability-Focused Communication*

1. **Define Roles and Responsibilities Clearly**

   o Use specific, measurable language when setting expectations, e.g., "Your goal is to complete this project by Friday," rather than "Complete it as soon as you can."

2. **Provide Constructive Feedback Regularly**

   o Make feedback an ongoing part of communication. Recognize achievements and address areas for improvement in a way that supports growth and builds mutual respect.

3. **Encourage Peer Accountability**

   o Cultivate a culture where team members feel comfortable providing constructive feedback to each other. Peer accountability promotes collective ownership and strengthens the team's commitment to shared goals.

## *Real-World Example: Accountability in a Product Development Team*

In a product development team, manager David implemented bi-weekly check-ins, where each member discussed their progress and challenges. By providing constructive feedback and encouraging team members to hold each other accountable, David created a culture of shared responsibility that led to higher productivity and innovation.

# *Decisiveness and Communication: Providing Clarity and Confidence*

## *The Role of Communication in Decisiveness*

Decisiveness in leadership is more than just making quick decisions; it's about providing clarity and direction that empower team members to act with confidence. Decisive communication removes ambiguity, allowing team members to understand and trust their leader's vision and expectations.

## *Techniques for Decisive Communication*

1. **Be Clear and Direct**

   o Avoid ambiguous language. Instead of saying, "We might consider this option," use decisive statements like "We'll go with this option because it best aligns with our goals."

2. **Outline the Rationale**

   o When making decisions, explain the reasoning behind your choice. This transparency builds trust and helps team members learn from your decision-making process.

3. **Encourage Independent Decision-Making**

   o Empower team members to make decisions in their areas of responsibility. Reinforce that they have the authority to act and support them when they take the initiative.

## *Real-World Example: Decisiveness in a Tech Start-Up*

Susie, a project manager at a tech start-up, noticed her team often hesitated to make decisions on small matters, leading to delays. By clearly outlining her decision-making process and setting parameters for independent decision-making, she empowered her team to act confidently. This approach increased efficiency and allowed the team to complete projects faster.

# *Building a Culture of Transparent Communication*

## *Why Transparency Matters*

Transparency in communication is essential for building trust. When leaders are open about goals, challenges, and changes, they foster a culture where team members feel included and valued. Transparent communication supports each LEAD principle by ensuring that information flows freely, which promotes connection, accountability, and autonomy.

## *Strategies for Fostering Transparency*

1. **Share Organizational Goals and Challenges**

   o   Regularly update your team on high-level goals and challenges the organization faces. This openness builds trust and helps team members align their efforts with larger objectives.

2. **Involve Team Members in Decisions**

   o   When possible, involve team members in decision-making, particularly for decisions that directly affect them. Involving them builds ownership and reinforces that their perspectives are valued.

### 3. Establish Open Channels for Communication

- ○ Create multiple avenues for team members to share feedback, such as anonymous suggestion boxes, regular check-ins, or open-door policies. Open channels encourage continuous dialogue and reinforce transparency.

## *Real-World Example: Transparency in a Financial Services Firm*

Lisa, a manager in a financial services firm, realized that her team felt disconnected from company goals. She began holding monthly meetings to share the firm's progress, challenges, and key decisions. This transparency improved team engagement, as team members felt more aligned with the company's mission and saw their contributions as part of the bigger picture.

# *Conclusion: Communication as the Foundation of LEAD*

Effective communication is at the heart of the **LEAD** Development Pathway, enabling leaders to integrate Listening, Empathy, Accountability, and Decisiveness into their approach. By using open, transparent communication, leaders build trust, clarity, and a strong foundation for adaptive leadership.

Through thoughtful communication strategies—such as asking open-ended questions, validating emotions, providing clear expectations, and encouraging autonomy—leaders can create an environment where team members feel connected, supported, and empowered to achieve their goals. As we move forward, **Chapter 7: Building a Culture of Trust with LEAD** will explore how trust is essential to adaptive leadership and how LEAD principles can foster a strong, collaborative team culture.

# *Chapter 7:*

# Building a Culture of Trust with LEAD

## *Introduction*

Trust is the cornerstone of any successful team. It creates a sense of psychological safety where team members feel confident to share ideas, voice concerns, and take initiative. For adaptive leaders, trust is especially critical, as it enables flexibility, openness to change, and a willingness to embrace challenges. Trust also reinforces each of the **LEAD** principles, as leaders who listen actively, show empathy, hold themselves and others accountable, and make clear decisions foster an environment of respect and reliability.

In this chapter, we'll explore how each LEAD principle contributes to building a culture of trust and provide practical techniques for leaders to cultivate trust within their teams. We'll also examine real-world examples that illustrate how trust impacts team performance and resilience.

## *Listening and Trust: Creating a Foundation of Respect*

### *Why Listening Builds Trust*

Listening is the most direct way to show respect and establish trust. When leaders listen actively, team members feel valued and respected, which, in turn, creates a sense of security and belonging. Listening fosters trust by showing that leaders care about team members' ideas and concerns, encouraging a free flow of communication.

## *Techniques for Building Trust Through Listening*

1. **Practice Active Listening in Every Interaction**

   o   Show full attention when team members speak. Nodding, maintaining eye contact, and avoiding interruptions demonstrate genuine interest and respect.

2. **Hold Regular Check-Ins**

   o   Schedule consistent one-on-one or team check-ins where team members can share updates, ideas, and concerns. Regular check-ins create a predictable, safe space for open dialogue.

3. **Implement an Open-Door Policy**

   o   Encourage team members to approach you with questions or feedback at any time. An open-door policy reinforces that their input is always welcome.

## *Real-World Example: Listening in Action in a Therapy Practice*

At a group practice, a clinical supervisor noticed his team members felt hesitant to share ideas during group meetings. He implemented weekly one-on-one check-ins where he asked open-ended questions and actively listened without judgment. Over time, this practice built a foundation of trust, encouraging team members to speak more openly, which led to more innovative solutions and team cohesion.

# *Empathy and Trust: Fostering a Supportive Environment*

### *The Role of Empathy in Building Trust*

Empathy strengthens trust by making team members feel seen, understood, and supported. When leaders show empathy, they create a safe environment where individuals feel comfortable expressing themselves honestly. Empathy fosters trust by validating team members' emotions, prioritizing their well-being.

### *Techniques for Building Trust Through Empathy*

1. **Acknowledge Personal and Professional Challenges**

   o Recognize when team members are facing stressors, both in and out of work. Simple acknowledgments, like "I know you have a lot on your plate," show understanding and build a supportive team environment.

2. **Create Opportunities for Open Emotional Expression**

   o   Encourage team members to share feelings related to work projects, challenges, or stress. Offering a space for emotional expression makes empathy a regular part of team culture.

3. **Offer Supportive Flexibility**

   o   Demonstrate empathy by offering flexible solutions when team members are under pressure, such as adjusting deadlines or redistributed tasks. Flexibility reinforces that you are responsive to their needs.

## *Real-World Example: Empathy at a University*

A university dean noticed her professors were stressed and experiencing burnout. She introduced "empathy hours," during which professors could share their challenges without fear of judgment. By validating their experiences and offering flexible schedules, she built a foundation of trust and support, which improved morale and reduced turnover.

# *Accountability and Trust: Building Reliability and Integrity*

## *Why Accountability Builds Trust*

Accountability is essential for creating a culture where team members know they can rely on each other. When leaders hold themselves and their teams accountable, they reinforce reliability, honesty, and mutual respect. Accountability-driven leaders build trust by setting clear expectations, following through on commitments, and promoting a fair, consistent environment.

## *Techniques for Building Trust Through Accountability*

1.  **Lead by Example**

    o   Model accountability by following through on your own commitments and acknowledging any mistakes you make. Leaders who admit their errors encourage others to be open about their own.

2.  **Set Clear Expectations**

    o   Define roles, responsibilities, and goals clearly so each team member understands their contributions and how they impact the team. Clarity in expectations strengthens trust by eliminating ambiguity.

3.  **Recognize and Celebrate Accountability**

    o   Acknowledge team members who take responsibility and meet commitments. Publicly celebrating accountability reinforces its value and encourages everyone to hold themselves to the same standard.

### *Real-World Example: Accountability in a Sales Team*

A sales manager noticed inconsistencies in performance and implemented weekly accountability check-ins, where each team member reported on their targets. By consistently reinforcing accountability and celebrating achievements, the manager fostered a reliability culture, strengthening trust and improving overall performance.

# *Decisiveness and Trust: Providing Stability and Confidence*

### *The Role of Decisiveness in Building Trust*

Decisive leaders instill trust by providing stability and clarity. When leaders make confident, transparent decisions, they reassure their team that they are prepared to lead and handle challenges. Decisiveness also shows that leaders have a clear vision and are committed to taking action, which helps team members feel secure and motivated.

### *Techniques for Building Trust Through Decisiveness*

1. **Make Decisions with Transparency**

   o When making decisions, explain the reasoning behind them. Transparency helps team members understand and trust the decision-making process, even if they may disagree with specific outcomes.

2. **Involve the Team When Possible**

   o When appropriate, consult team members in decision-making, particularly on issues that directly impact them. Team involvement fosters a sense of ownership and reinforces trust in the leader's commitment to inclusivity.

3. **Provide Consistent Follow-Through**

   o After making a decision, ensure consistent follow-through to demonstrate commitment. A leader who follows through on their decisions builds credibility and reinforces that they can be trusted.

## *Real-World Example: Decisiveness in a Manufacturing Plant*

A production supervisor faced delays in the manufacturing process due to unforeseen supply chain issues. He maintained his team's confidence and trust by making quick, decisive adjustments to the production schedule and explaining the reasoning behind these changes. His decisiveness provided stability and helped the team adapt quickly to the new plan.

# *Practical Steps to Build and Sustain Trust with LEAD*

Building trust is not a one-time effort; it's a continuous process that requires consistency, communication, and respect. Here are some additional strategies to help leaders foster and maintain trust over time:

1. **Encourage Open Dialogue at All Levels**

   o   Establish open lines of communication where team members feel comfortable sharing ideas or feedback. This culture of open dialogue supports trust-building by reinforcing that all perspectives are valued.

2. **Be Transparent About Organizational Goals**

   o   Regularly update the team on organizational goals, challenges, and changes. Transparency helps team members feel aligned with the bigger picture, fostering a shared sense of purpose and commitment.

3. **Practice Humility and Openness to Feedback**

   o   Leaders who are open to feedback and willing to admit their limitations demonstrate humility, which strengthens trust. Leaders set an example of authenticity by showing that they are learning and evolving.

4. **Provide Opportunities for Team-Building**

   o   Organize team-building activities that allow team members to connect in a non-work context. Strong interpersonal relationships within the team support a trusting, collaborative environment.

5. **Celebrate Team Successes**

   o Recognize and celebrate team achievements, no matter how small. Acknowledging success builds morale, reinforces the importance of each team member's contributions, and deepens trust.

# *Conclusion: Trust as the Foundation of LEAD*

Trust is at the core of adaptive leadership, allowing leaders to apply **Listening, Empathy, Accountability,** and **Decisiveness** in a way that resonates with and empowers their team. By consistently applying these principles, leaders create a culture where team members feel respected, valued, and motivated to work collaboratively toward shared goals.

Trust enables a team to adapt to change, embrace challenges, and perform at their highest potential. As we move into **Chapter 8: LEAD in Team Development and Cohesion**, we'll explore how the LEAD framework can be applied to strengthen team cohesion, unity, and mutual support as teams progress through their development journey.

# *Chapter 8:*

# LEAD in Team Development and Cohesion

## *Introduction*

Team cohesion refers to the connection, trust, and unity level among team members. Cohesive teams are more resilient, productive, and better equipped to navigate challenges together. Leaders who prioritize cohesion create an environment where team members feel supported, valued, and motivated to work toward shared goals.

The **LEAD** framework—**Listening, Empathy, Accountability, and Decisiveness**—plays a vital role in building and sustaining team cohesion. Each principle addresses a specific aspect of team dynamics, enabling leaders to strengthen relationships, encourage mutual support, and foster a culture where everyone is aligned and committed. In this chapter, we'll discuss how each LEAD principle supports team development and cohesion and strategies for reinforcing these principles within a team.

# *Listening and Team Development: Building Connection and Unity*

## *Why Listening Supports Team Cohesion*

Listening is essential for creating a culture of openness and connection within a team. When leaders listen actively, they show that each team member's voice matters, fostering an environment where everyone feels comfortable sharing insights and concerns. Active listening among team members enhances understanding and reduces miscommunication, which is vital for unity and cohesion.

## *Techniques for Enhancing Cohesion Through Listening*

1. **Encourage Team Members to Listen to Each Other**

   o Promote listening as a team value by encouraging members to listen actively during discussions. Reinforce that understanding each other's perspectives is key to building a supportive environment.

2. **Facilitate Open Dialogues and Brainstorming Sessions**

   o Regularly hold sessions where team members can share ideas or feedback. Open dialogues create a space where team members can contribute without fear of judgment, fostering a sense of collective ownership.

### 3. Use Active Listening Exercises

- Incorporate exercises that build active listening skills. For example, pair team members and have one share an idea while the other listens without interrupting and then summarizes what they heard. This builds understanding and encourages mutual respect.

## *Real-World Example: Building Unity with Active Listening in a Design Team*

A design manager implemented weekly brainstorming sessions where team members took turns sharing ideas without interruptions. This practice improved team members' listening skills, helped them understand each other's viewpoints, and encouraged collaboration, which led to more cohesive project outcomes.

# *Empathy and Team Development: Creating a Supportive Team Environment*

## *The Role of Empathy in Fostering Cohesion*

Empathy is essential for developing a supportive and connected team. When team members feel understood and supported, they are more likely to form strong, positive relationships with one another. Empathy-driven leaders foster a culture where individuals feel comfortable sharing their challenges, knowing they will receive compassion and assistance from both their leader and peers.

## *Techniques for Enhancing Cohesion Through Empathy*

1. **Encourage Peer Support**

   o Promote a culture where team members check in with each other and offer support during high-stress periods. Peer support builds a sense of camaraderie and shared resilience.

2. **Model Empathetic Behavior**

   o Demonstrate empathy consistently so that team members are encouraged to follow suit. Empathetic leaders who openly acknowledge and support their team members' emotions create a foundation of mutual respect.

3. **Recognize and Validate Team Members' Experiences**

   o Publicly acknowledge individual or collective challenges the team has faced. Recognizing shared experiences strengthens bonds and encourages team members to rely on each other.

## *Real-World Example: Building a Supportive Environment in a Health Clinic*

A team lead at a busy health clinic noticed her staff struggling with patient overload. She encouraged team members to support each other, regularly checked in, and validated their efforts publicly. This practice helped the team develop a strong sense of unity and support, which increased resilience and morale.

# *Accountability and Team Development: Strengthening Mutual Responsibility*

## *How Accountability Fosters Cohesion*

Accountability promotes reliability, consistency, and a sense of collective responsibility among team members. In a cohesive team, individuals take ownership of their roles, knowing their contributions impact the group's success. Leaders who emphasize accountability help team members understand that they are responsible to themselves and each other.

## *Techniques for Enhancing Cohesion Through Accountability*

1. **Establish Shared Goals and Expectations**

   o Set clear, collective goals that require each team member's contributions. Shared goals emphasize that the team's success depends on everyone's accountability.

2. **Encourage Collaborative Problem-Solving**

   o When challenges arise, encourage team members to work together to find solutions. Collaborative problem-solving promotes shared ownership and reinforces a sense of responsibility to the team.

3. **Introduce Team Accountability Check-Ins**

   o Implement periodic check-ins where team members discuss their progress toward goals and identify areas where they may need support. These check-ins reinforce mutual accountability and build trust.

## *Real-World Example: Accountability in an Operations Team*

An operations manager sets monthly team goals rather than individual ones, encouraging everyone to support each other in reaching targets. He fostered a strong sense of shared responsibility and unity by holding the team collectively accountable, leading to higher performance and morale.

# *Decisiveness and Team Development: Providing Clarity and Encouraging Ownership*

## *Why Decisiveness Builds Team Cohesion*

Decisive leaders provide stability, confidence, and direction, which helps unify team members around shared objectives. Team members feel secure and aligned when leaders make clear decisions and communicate openly. Decisiveness also encourages team members to take ownership of their roles, fostering independence within a cohesive structure.

# *Techniques for Enhancing Cohesion Through Decisiveness*

1. **Be Transparent in Decision-Making**

   o Share the reasons behind major decisions, emphasizing how each decision supports the team's goals. Transparency creates alignment and reinforces the team's purpose.

2. **Encourage Team Members to Make Decisions Together**

   o Involve the team in decision-making for projects that impact them directly. Collaborative decision-making strengthens cohesion by reinforcing that each member has a voice.

3. **Promote Ownership Through Delegation**

   o Delegate responsibilities and allow team members to make decisions within their roles. Trusting them with responsibility encourages autonomy and reinforces the team's shared objectives.

# *Real-World Example: Decisiveness in a Food Service Team*

At a local steakhouse, a team leader made it a practice to involve her team in key decision-making for the restaurant. By trusting team members to make certain decisions, she fostered a sense of ownership and pride in the group's work, creating a united team culture.

# *Practical Strategies for Sustaining Team Cohesion*

Building and sustaining team cohesion requires intentionality and commitment. Here are some strategies to maintain and strengthen team unity over time:

1. **Hold Regular Team-Building Activities**

   o Plan activities where team members can connect outside of work tasks. Informal interactions strengthen bonds and make collaborating easier for team members.

2. **Celebrate Shared Milestones and Successes**

   o Acknowledge collective achievements, no matter how small. Celebrating wins reinforces that each member's contributions are valued and essential to the team's success.

3. **Encourage Knowledge Sharing and Cross-Training**

   o Foster an environment where team members can learn from each other and share skills. Cross-training strengthens the team's capabilities and builds connections between team members.

4. **Promote Consistent, Open Communication**

- o Keep communication lines open, encouraging team members to discuss both positive developments and challenges. Consistent communication supports ongoing trust and alignment.

5. **Foster a Growth Mindset**

   - o Encourage team members to view challenges as opportunities for learning and improvement. A growth mindset promotes resilience and unity, as team members support each other in facing obstacles together.

# *Conclusion: LEAD Principles as Pillars of Team Cohesion*

Each LEAD principle—**Listening, Empathy, Accountability, and Decisiveness**—is integral to building a cohesive, high-performing team. By actively applying these principles, leaders can foster an environment of mutual respect, support, and collaboration. Cohesion does not happen by accident; it is built through intentional practices that encourage team members to connect, support one another, and work toward shared goals.

A cohesive team is more resilient, adaptable, and aligned, allowing them to handle challenges and capitalize on opportunities together.

# Chapter 9:
# Applying LEAD in Remote Work Environments

## *Introduction*

Remote work has transformed the way teams communicate, collaborate, and connect. Without the benefit of in-person interactions, remote leaders must rely on virtual tools to foster relationships, maintain accountability, and drive productivity. The LEAD framework—**Listening, Empathy, Accountability, and Decisiveness**—is especially valuable in remote settings, where these qualities can bridge physical gaps and support a cohesive, high-performing team. This section provides specific strategies for applying each LEAD principle in a remote work environment.

## *Listening in a Remote Setting*

### *Challenges*

Remote work can create barriers to communication, with team members often feeling isolated or hesitant to share concerns over virtual platforms. Without face-to-face cues, leaders must actively foster an environment that encourages open dialogue and authentic connection.

## *Strategies for Remote Listening*

### 1. Schedule Regular Check-Ins

○ Set up weekly or bi-weekly one-on-one video calls with team members to discuss their workload, address challenges, and offer support. These sessions are essential for creating space where team members feel comfortable sharing.

### 2. Use Collaborative Platforms for Open Feedback

○ Implement online tools for ongoing conversations, allowing team members to share ideas, ask questions, and offer feedback in real time.

### 3. Show Presence and Engagement

○ Demonstrate active listening during virtual meetings by keeping your camera on, maintaining eye contact, and providing feedback or follow-up questions. Simple actions like nodding or summarizing key points help team members feel heard and valued.

# *Empathy in a Remote Setting*

## *Challenges*

The lack of in-person interaction can make it difficult for leaders to pick up on non-verbal cues that indicate stress or disengagement. Remote employees may also struggle with balancing work and personal life, which can impact their well-being.

## *Strategies for Remote Empathy*

1. **Acknowledge Remote Work Realities**

   - Recognize the unique challenges of remote work, such as potential feelings of isolation, screen fatigue, and the need for work-life balance. Let team members know that you understand these pressures.

2. **Encourage Flexibility**

   - When possible, offer flexible hours that allow team members to work when they're most productive or attend to personal responsibilities. This flexibility demonstrates empathy and supports well-being.

3. **Check-In on Well-Being**

   - Use tools like surveys or brief virtual check-ins to assess team members' well-being and stress levels. Show empathy by addressing concerns and offering support where needed, such as adjusting workloads during particularly stressful periods.

# *Accountability in a Remote Setting*

## *Challenges*

Remote work can make monitoring performance difficult, and accountability may weaken without regular in-person interactions. Leaders need clear systems to track progress and set expectations without resorting to micromanagement.

## *Strategies for Remote Accountability*

1. **Set Clear Goals and Milestones**

   - Define measurable goals for each project and establish regular milestones to track progress. Share these expectations openly so everyone knows their responsibilities and deadlines.

2. **Use Project Management Tools**

   - Implement tools to organize tasks, deadlines, and responsibilities. Electronic platforms help everyone stay on track and provide visibility into each team member's contributions.

3. **Encourage Peer Accountability**

   - Create opportunities for team members to review each other's work, collaborate on tasks, and provide feedback. This approach promotes accountability within the team while reducing the need for leader oversight.

# *Decisiveness in a Remote Setting*

## *Challenges*

Remote teams often work across different locations and time zones, which can slow down decision-making. Leaders need to be decisive to maintain momentum and provide clarity, even when full consensus is challenging.

## *Strategies for Remote Decisiveness*

1. **Make Timely Decisions, Communicate Clearly**

   o   Avoid delays by making informed decisions with the information available. Once a decision is made, communicate it clearly through a central channel and explain the rationale to keep everyone aligned.

2. **Empower Team Members to Make Decisions**

   o   Delegate decision-making authority for certain projects or tasks to remote team members. Encourage them to make choices independently, fostering confidence and reducing dependency on leadership.

3. **Embrace Asynchronous Communication**

   o   Recognize that remote teams may not always be available for immediate feedback. Use asynchronous tools like project boards or shared documents to keep progress visible and allow team members to move forward without waiting for real-time responses.

## *Conclusion: Leveraging LEAD for Remote Team Success*

Applying the LEAD framework in a remote work environment requires adapting traditional approaches to suit virtual interactions. By focusing on **active listening, empathetic flexibility, structured accountability,** and **timely decisiveness**, remote leaders can cultivate a collaborative, high-trust culture. Even in a virtual setting, LEAD principles empower teams to perform at their best, fostering connection and productivity despite physical distance.

# *Chapter 10:*

# LEAD and Conflict Resolution: Building Resilience in Teams

## *Introduction*

Conflict is a natural part of any team environment. It can lead to stronger relationships, innovative solutions, and personal growth when managed effectively. Adaptive leaders recognize that how they handle conflicts significantly impacts team dynamics and morale. By applying **Listening, Empathy, Accountability,** and **Decisiveness,** leaders can turn potentially divisive situations into opportunities for growth and resilience.

In this chapter, we'll explore how each LEAD principle can be applied to resolve conflicts, foster understanding, and build a team culture where challenges are seen as chances for development.

## *Listening and Conflict Resolution: Creating Understanding*

### *How Listening Helps Resolve Conflict*

Listening is essential for understanding the root causes of conflict. Often, disagreements stem from miscommunications, unmet expectations, or misunderstandings. Leaders who practice active listening can uncover underlying issues and create an environment where all parties feel heard. This foundation of understanding helps de-escalate tensions and fosters a respectful, open atmosphere.

## *Techniques for Conflict Resolution Through Listening*

1. **Listen Without Interruption**

   o Allow each team member involved in the conflict to share their perspective fully before responding. Avoid interrupting or making assumptions.

2. **Use Reflective Listening**

   o Summarize or paraphrase what each person said to ensure you understand their viewpoint. Reflective listening reassures team members that their concerns are being taken seriously.

3. **Ask Clarifying Questions**

   o Use open-ended questions like "Can you tell me more about what you were hoping to achieve?" to clarify specific details and promote deeper understanding.

## *Real-World Example: Listening to De-Escalate*

A manager observed rising tensions between two team members due to competing sales territories. By holding individual listening sessions with each person, the manager gained a better understanding of their motivations and frustrations. He then held a joint session, where both members shared their perspectives. This listening-centered approach led to a compromise that improved teamwork and restored a positive working environment.

# *Empathy and Conflict Resolution: Fostering Emotional Safety*

## *The Role of Empathy in Managing Conflict*

Empathy helps create a safe space for team members to express emotions without fear of judgment. By showing empathy, leaders validate team members' feelings, which can reduce defensiveness and open the door to constructive dialogue. Empathy is crucial in transforming conflict from a source of division into an opportunity for connection and understanding.

## *Techniques for Conflict Resolution Through Empathy*

1. **Acknowledge Emotions**

   o Recognize and validate team members' emotions with statements like, "I can see this situation has been frustrating for you." Validating emotions can help reduce anger and encourage openness.

2. **Encourage Emotional Expression**

   o Encourage team members to express how the conflict has impacted them personally. This allows for a release of emotions and promotes mutual understanding.

3. **Show Compassionate Body Language**

   o Display empathy through non-verbal cues, such as nodding, maintaining eye contact, and showing an open posture. Compassionate body language signals that you genuinely care about their concerns.

## *Real-World Example: Using Empathy in Conflict Resolution*

A school principal noticed tension between two teachers over shared resources. In a private meeting, she encouraged each teacher to share their frustrations and validated their feelings. By showing empathy, she created a safe space where both teachers felt supported. This empathy-driven approach helped them understand each other's perspectives, which led to a collaborative solution.

# *Accountability and Conflict Resolution: Establishing Responsibility and Fairness*

## *Why Accountability is Key in Conflict Resolution*

Accountability helps clarify expectations and establish boundaries, ensuring that team members understand their responsibilities in resolving conflicts. Leaders who emphasize accountability create a fair environment where individuals are held responsible for their actions and behavior. Accountability also prevents recurring conflicts by reinforcing team values and standards.

# *Techniques for Conflict Resolution Through Accountability*

1. **Define Clear Boundaries and Responsibilities**

   - Outline specific responsibilities for each person involved, clarifying what is expected moving forward. Accountability in conflict resolution often involves creating agreements to prevent future issues.

2. **Hold All Parties Accountable**

   - If multiple team members are involved in the conflict, ensure that each person takes responsibility for their role in the situation. Fair accountability fosters trust and prevents favoritism.

3. **Follow Up Regularly**

   - Schedule follow-up meetings to assess progress, revisit agreements, and address any lingering concerns. Consistent follow-up demonstrates a commitment to resolving conflicts fairly and thoroughly.

# *Real-World Example: Accountability in Resolving Conflict*

A marketing manager noticed that two team members were clashing over creative direction on a project. He established a clear action plan after meeting with both members to discuss their roles and expectations. He held both team members accountable for adhering to the agreed-upon direction and followed up weekly. This structured approach resolved the conflict and reinforced accountability, leading to a more harmonious working relationship.

# *Decisiveness and Conflict Resolution: Providing Clarity and Moving Forward*

## *The Role of Decisiveness in Resolving Conflict*

Decisive leadership is essential for addressing conflict promptly and establishing a clear path forward. Leaders who are decisive in conflict resolution create confidence in their ability to guide the team through challenges. Decisiveness also prevents conflicts from festering, allowing the team to focus on collaborative progress rather than unresolved issues.

## *Techniques for Conflict Resolution Through Decisiveness*

1. **Act Promptly**

   o Address conflicts as soon as they arise to prevent escalation. Delayed action can lead to misunderstandings, resentment, and a breakdown in team trust.

2. **Make Clear, Fair Decisions**

   o Evaluate all perspectives, then make a balanced decision that aligns with team goals and values.

Avoid ambiguous resolutions that may leave the issue unresolved.

3. **Communicate the Resolution Clearly**

   o Once a decision is made, clearly and transparently communicate it to all parties involved. Clear communication reduces the risk of misinterpretation and allows the team to move forward.

### *Real-World Example: Decisiveness in Conflict Resolution*

At a program start-up, a project manager encountered a conflict between developers over the technical approach to a software project. Recognizing the impact of the delay, the manager made a prompt decision after hearing both perspectives. He provided a clear rationale and communicated the final approach to the team, emphasizing the need for unity and collaboration. This decisive action prevented further delays and restored the team's focus.

# *Integrating LEAD Principles for Lasting Conflict Resolution*

When combined, the LEAD principles offer a comprehensive approach to conflict resolution that prioritizes understanding, fairness, and progress. Leaders who integrate all four principles can resolve conflicts constructively, prevent future disputes, and build a team culture where challenges strengthen rather than weaken relationships.

## *Practical Steps for Resolving Conflicts with LEAD*

1. **Conduct a LEAD Conflict Resolution Meeting**

   o   Hold a structured meeting where each principle is applied. Start by listening to each person's perspective, showing empathy for their experiences, clarifying roles and responsibilities, and making a clear decision on the resolution.

2. **Create Conflict Resolution Agreements**

   o   Develop agreements based on accountability, detailing what each person will commit to moving forward. These agreements should be documented and revisited regularly.

3. **Promote a Growth Mindset**

   o   Encourage team members to view conflicts as learning experiences. A growth mindset fosters resilience and reminds the team that challenges offer valuable insights for improvement.

4. **Provide Conflict Resolution Training**

   o   Offer training on conflict resolution techniques, emphasizing the importance of active listening, empathy, and accountability. This empowers team members to manage minor conflicts independently, promoting a self-sustaining, resilient culture.

# *Conclusion: LEAD as a Framework for Resilient Conflict Resolution*

Conflict, when approached constructively, can become a source of growth and resilience for teams. The LEAD framework—**Listening, Empathy, Accountability,** and **Decisiveness**—provides a roadmap for handling conflicts to strengthen relationships, clarify responsibilities, and promote unity.

By applying LEAD principles, leaders transform conflicts from divisive events into opportunities for deeper understanding, trust, and cohesion. As we continue to **Chapter 11: The Future of Adaptive Leadership and LEAD**, we will explore how the LEAD framework will evolve to meet the needs of a changing workforce, technological advances, and cross-cultural teams.

# *Chapter 11:*

# The Future of Adaptive Leadership and LEAD

## *Introduction*

The workplace is evolving at an unprecedented pace. Remote work, digital transformation, and increasingly diverse global teams have introduced new challenges and opportunities for leaders. Adaptive leadership has never been more critical, as leaders must constantly adjust their approaches to stay relevant and effective in these changing environments.

The **LEAD** framework—**Listening, Empathy, Accountability, and Decisiveness**—offers a versatile toolkit that supports adaptive leadership in this evolving context. By applying LEAD principles thoughtfully, leaders can embrace flexibility, connect with team members across distances and cultures, and foster trust in a rapidly transforming world.

This chapter will examine how LEAD principles can be adapted to meet the unique demands of emerging workplace trends, ensuring that leaders are prepared to guide their teams successfully into the future.

# *Technological Advances and LEAD: Leveraging Innovation for Effective Leadership*

## *Challenges and Opportunities with Technology*

New technologies such as artificial intelligence, data analytics, and collaboration tools offer leaders opportunities to enhance productivity and decision-making. However, leaders must also address potential challenges, such as data overload, technology-driven isolation, and the need to balance human interaction with automation.

## *Applying LEAD Principles in a Tech-Driven Environment*

1. **Listening**: Use tools like anonymous surveys and data analytics to gather feedback from team members on their experiences with new technologies. Listening helps leaders make informed adjustments and ensure that technology aligns with team needs.

2. **Empathy**: Recognize that team members may experience anxiety or resistance to new technology. Leaders can ease this transition by offering support, training, and time to adapt to technological changes.

3. **Accountability**: Set clear expectations for how technology will be used, including guidelines on data security, response times, and digital communication

etiquette. These boundaries help maintain professionalism and responsibility.

4. **Decisiveness**: Evaluate new technologies quickly and make informed decisions about adoption. Leaders should weigh the potential benefits and risks and then act decisively to implement or adjust tech strategies as needed.

## *Real-World Example: Implementing AI in a Financial Services Team*

A financial services firm introduced AI tools to automate data analysis. The manager applied LEAD principles by gathering feedback on the AI system (Listening), addressing initial resistance with training (Empathy), clarifying accountability for data use (Accountability), and making swift adjustments based on team feedback (Decisiveness). This approach ensured a smooth transition to AI-driven processes, enhancing productivity and team satisfaction.

# *Cross-Cultural Teams and LEAD: Embracing Diversity and Fostering Inclusion*

### *The Importance of Cross-Cultural Leadership*

As globalization connects teams across borders, leaders must navigate cultural differences in communication, work styles, and values. Effective cross-cultural leadership respects diversity while promoting inclusivity and unity, creating an environment where all team members feel valued.

## *Applying LEAD Principles to Cross-Cultural Teams*

1. **Listening**: Practice active listening to understand cultural perspectives, customs, and preferences. Leaders should ask open-ended questions to learn about team members' values, work styles, and communication needs.

2. **Empathy**: Show empathy by acknowledging cultural differences and respecting each team member's background. Leaders can celebrate cultural holidays, observe diverse practices, and provide resources on cultural awareness to promote inclusivity.

3. **Accountability**: Establish consistent, inclusive standards that ensure fairness and respect across cultures. Clear guidelines for collaboration, language use, and feedback practices foster a cohesive and respectful environment.

4. **Decisiveness**: Make inclusive decisions that account for diverse perspectives, avoiding one-size-fits-all solutions. Decisive leaders are careful to avoid cultural biases in decision-making and strive to accommodate varied viewpoints.

## *Real-World Example: Cross-Cultural Leadership in a For-Profit Agency*

A for-profit agency with team members from multiple countries applied LEAD principles to promote inclusivity. Regular cross-cultural team meetings supported listening, empathy was shown through cultural awareness sessions, accountability was reinforced by establishing inclusive collaboration guidelines, and decisiveness was practiced by ensuring that all decisions considered diverse viewpoints. These practices enhanced cohesion and productivity within the multicultural team.

# The Rise of Soft Skills and LEAD: Prioritizing Emotional Intelligence and Human Connection

## The Growing Importance of Soft Skills

In a world increasingly shaped by technology, soft skills like emotional intelligence, adaptability, and effective communication are essential for leaders. The ability to connect with team members on a human level supports engagement, motivation, and resilience in a fast-paced, changing environment.

## Applying LEAD Principles to Develop Soft Skills

1. **Listening**: Leaders should refine their listening skills to fully understand and appreciate team members' perspectives, concerns, and motivations. Listening builds rapport and fosters a sense of belonging.

2. **Empathy**: Empathy has become a central leadership skill, as it helps leaders connect authentically with team

members. By recognizing and validating emotions, leaders strengthen team morale and engagement.

3. **Accountability**: Soft skills like responsibility and integrity are critical in an evolving workplace. Leaders who model accountability and encourage it among team members create a culture of reliability and trust.

4. **Decisiveness**: Adaptability and clear decision-making are essential soft skills for leaders facing rapid changes. Decisive leaders who communicate transparently help teams navigate uncertainty with confidence.

## *Real-World Example: Soft Skills in an Educational Institution*

A university's department head focused on developing soft skills by incorporating LEAD principles. She practiced active listening to understand faculty concerns, demonstrated empathy during stressful academic seasons, emphasized accountability through regular progress check-ins, and made clear decisions during curriculum changes. This approach fostered an environment where faculty felt supported and motivated, improving both collaboration and morale.

# *Sustainability and LEAD: Leading with a Long-Term Vision*

## *Leadership in an Era of Social Responsibility*

Today's leaders are increasingly expected to prioritize sustainability and social responsibility. This shift reflects a growing awareness of environmental, social, and governance (ESG) concerns and a commitment to creating a positive impact. Leaders who adopt a sustainable approach build trust, foster loyalty, and align their teams with a long-term vision.

## *Applying LEAD Principles to Support Sustainability*

1. **Listening**: Gather insights from team members about sustainability practices and their impact. Leaders who listen to their team's perspectives on social responsibility can make more informed and inclusive decisions.

2. **Empathy**: Show empathy by considering business practices' social and environmental impact. Leaders who prioritize sustainable values create an ethical, purpose-driven team culture.

3. **Accountability**: Establish clear sustainability goals and hold team members accountable for contributing to these objectives. Accountability in sustainability encourages responsible decision-making and long-term commitment.

4. **Decisiveness**: Make timely, informed decisions about sustainability initiatives. Leaders must act decisively to support sustainable practices, balancing immediate needs with long-term impact.

## *Real-World Example: Sustainability in a Retail Company*

A retail company committed to sustainability applied LEAD principles to drive its initiatives. Management conducted surveys

(Listening) to understand employees' views on sustainability, showed empathy by addressing concerns about supply chain practices, reinforced accountability by setting measurable sustainability goals, and acted decisively by implementing eco-friendly packaging solutions. These practices aligned the team with the company's sustainable vision and fostered a sense of purpose.

# Conclusion: LEAD as an Adaptive Leadership Framework for the Future

As the workplace evolves, adaptive leadership becomes essential for navigating remote work, technological advancements, diverse teams, and a stronger focus on sustainability and soft skills. The **LEAD** framework—**Listening, Empathy, Accountability,** and **Decisiveness**—remains a timeless and versatile approach that leaders can rely on to guide their teams successfully through these changes.

**By embracing the adaptability of LEAD principles,** leaders can respond to emerging challenges with resilience, empathy, and strategic clarity. The LEAD framework empowers leaders to foster connection, trust, and shared purpose in any environment—whether managing remote teams, integrating new technologies, or leading a culturally diverse workforce.

As the nature of work continues to change, LEAD will serve as a guiding foundation for leaders who wish to inspire, engage, and support their teams. By integrating **Listening, Empathy, Accountability,** and **Decisiveness** into everyday practices, leaders can create a future-oriented culture where adaptability and collaboration are cornerstones of success.

In the next chapter, **Chapter 12: Sustaining LEAD for Long-Term Success**, we'll explore strategies for embedding LEAD principles into team culture over time, ensuring that these values become a lasting part of the organization's DNA. Sustaining LEAD principles requires consistent reinforcement, development opportunities, and a commitment to continuous improvement.

# *Chapter 12:*

# Sustaining LEAD for Long-Term Success

## *Introduction*

The LEAD framework—**Listening, Empathy, Accountability, and Decisiveness**—is a powerful model for fostering adaptive, people-centered leadership. However, for these principles to have a lasting impact, leaders must ensure that LEAD values are deeply embedded in the team culture. Sustaining LEAD requires commitment, regular reinforcement, and a proactive approach to continuous improvement.

In this chapter, we'll cover strategies that help leaders integrate LEAD into the fabric of their team's daily operations, from setting clear expectations and celebrating milestones to providing ongoing development opportunities. By making LEAD principles a consistent part of team culture, leaders create an environment where adaptability, trust, and collaboration can flourish long-term.

## *1. Reinforce LEAD Principles Regularly*

### *Why Regular Reinforcement Matters*

Even the most effective leadership frameworks can fade over time without regular reinforcement. Leaders must consistently highlight and celebrate these values to maintain LEAD principles as guiding forces. Regular reinforcement ensures team members stay aligned with LEAD practices and encourages them to incorporate these principles into their work.

## *Techniques for Reinforcing LEAD Principles*

1. **Incorporate LEAD into Meetings**

   o Begin each team meeting with a brief focus on one of the LEAD principles. For example, dedicate a few minutes to discussing recent examples of team members who demonstrated effective listening, empathy, accountability, or decisiveness. This practice keeps LEAD principles at the forefront of team members' minds and encourages them to be applied in their interactions.

2. **Create LEAD-Focused Recognition Programs**

   o Recognize and reward team members who embody LEAD values in their daily work. For example, introduce "LEAD Champion" awards, where team members nominate peers who have exemplified one or more LEAD principles. This recognition motivates team members to adopt and sustain LEAD practices.

3. **Highlight LEAD in Company Communications**

   o Incorporate LEAD language and examples into company newsletters, updates, or internal communications. By embedding LEAD principles into official communications, leaders reinforce that these values are integral to the organization's mission and culture.

### *Real-World Example: LEAD-Focused Meeting Structure*

A customer service team leader began each weekly meeting by asking team members to share examples of when they saw LEAD principles in action. This practice kept LEAD at the forefront of the mind and created a sense of pride and unity among team members who saw their values reflected in each other's actions.

# 2. Set Clear LEAD-Aligned Goals and Expectations

## *The Role of LEAD in Goal-Setting*

When team goals align with LEAD principles, they provide clarity and direction, reinforcing the framework's values. By setting goals that explicitly incorporate **Listening, Empathy, Accountability,** and **Decisiveness**, leaders communicate that LEAD practices are central to team and organizational success.

## *Techniques for Setting LEAD-Aligned Goals*

1. **Incorporate LEAD into Performance Metrics**

   o Define specific, measurable goals that align with each LEAD principle. For example, a team goal might include "improving customer satisfaction by 20% through active listening" or

> "increasing team accountability by implementing weekly progress check-ins."

2. **Align LEAD Goals with Organizational Vision**

   o Ensure that LEAD-aligned goals reflect the organization's mission and vision. Leaders strengthen the relevance of these values by linking LEAD principles with broader organizational objectives.

3. **Review LEAD Goals Regularly**

   o Conduct quarterly or bi-annual reviews to assess progress toward LEAD-aligned goals. Regular review sessions allow teams to evaluate their progress, identify areas for improvement, and stay focused on maintaining LEAD practices.

## *Real-World Example: LEAD-Aligned Goals in a Communications Team*

A communications team sets quarterly goals based on LEAD principles, such as increasing accountability through collaborative project management tools and improving client relationships through empathetic communication. Regularly revisiting these goals helped the team stay focused on integrating LEAD values into every project.

# 3. Celebrate Milestones and Progress

## The Importance of Celebrating LEAD Milestones

Celebrating milestones and progress reinforces the importance of LEAD principles and motivates team members to continue their commitment to these values. Acknowledging progress boosts morale, fosters a sense of shared achievement, and highlights the tangible benefits of LEAD.

## Techniques for Celebrating LEAD Milestones

1. **Recognize Individual and Team Contributions**

   - Celebrate team members who go above and beyond in demonstrating LEAD principles. This can be done publicly during team meetings or with recognition awards that highlight their contributions.

2. **Celebrate LEAD Success Stories**

   - Share stories of how LEAD practices led to specific successes, such as resolving a client issue through empathetic listening or improving team performance through enhanced accountability. Success stories demonstrate the real impact of LEAD on team outcomes.

3. **Hold LEAD-Focused Events**

   o Organize team-building events, lunches, or workshops centered around celebrating LEAD values. These events provide an opportunity to reinforce LEAD principles in a relaxed, interactive setting, strengthening team cohesion.

### *Real-World Example: LEAD Success Stories*

An engineering team regularly celebrated "LEAD Success Stories" during monthly meetings, where team members shared examples of LEAD principles in action. This celebration boosted morale and inspired team members to adopt similar practices, reinforcing the value of LEAD over time.

# 4. Provide Continuous Development Opportunities

### *The Role of Continuous Learning in Sustaining LEAD*

Sustaining LEAD principles requires continuous learning and skill-building. By providing ongoing development opportunities, leaders can deepen team members' understanding of LEAD values and equip them with new techniques for applying these principles in dynamic situations.

# *Techniques for Continuous Development in LEAD*

1. **Offer LEAD-Specific Training**

   o Conduct workshops, seminars, or online courses that focus on skills related to **Listening, Empathy, Accountability,** and **Decisiveness**. Training sessions reinforce these principles and introduce practical strategies for applying them.

2. **Encourage Peer Learning**

   o Organize peer-led sessions where team members can share insights on how they've applied LEAD principles in their roles. Peer learning fosters a culture of shared knowledge and mutual support, sustaining LEAD values as team members learn from one another.

3. **Promote Leadership Development Programs**

   o For team members who show an interest in leadership, provide opportunities to develop their own LEAD-aligned leadership skills. This prepares future leaders who are already committed to maintaining the organization's LEAD culture.

### *Real-World Example: LEAD Workshops*

A healthcare organization conducted quarterly LEAD workshops focused on listening and empathy to improve patient care and team dynamics. These workshops helped reinforce LEAD principles across all levels of staff, creating a unified approach to patient-centered care.

# 5. Foster a Culture of Feedback and Improvement

### *The Importance of Feedback in Sustaining LEAD*

Feedback is essential for maintaining a culture that supports continuous improvement. Leaders who encourage regular feedback create an environment where team members feel empowered to suggest changes, share their experiences with LEAD, and identify areas for growth. This feedback-driven approach helps ensure that LEAD principles evolve alongside the team's needs.

### *Techniques for a Feedback-Driven Culture*

1. **Encourage Open Feedback Channels**

   o Create multiple channels for team members to provide feedback on LEAD practices. Anonymous surveys, feedback forms, or open-door policies allow team members to share honest insights, which helps leaders adjust LEAD practices as needed.

2. **Hold Regular LEAD Reflection Sessions**

   o Schedule periodic sessions where the team reflects on how well LEAD principles are being implemented. These sessions provide an opportunity to identify successes, address challenges, and reinforce a collective commitment to LEAD.

3. **Incorporate Feedback into LEAD Practices**

   o Act on the feedback received by making adjustments to existing practices or implementing new initiatives. Leaders who adapt based on feedback demonstrate a commitment to continuous improvement and create a culture where LEAD principles can evolve.

## *Real-World Example: Reflection Sessions in a Start-Up*

A start-up team held monthly "LEAD Reflection Sessions" where team members discussed what was working and what needed improvement in their application of LEAD principles. These sessions created a culture of openness and helped the team stay aligned with LEAD values in a fast-paced environment.

# *Conclusion: Sustaining LEAD as a Core Team Value*

Sustaining the LEAD framework—**Listening, Empathy, Accountability,** and **Decisiveness**—requires consistent reinforcement, a celebration of progress, and a commitment to ongoing improvement. By embedding LEAD principles into every aspect of team culture, from goal-setting to feedback, leaders ensure that these values become integral to how the team operates and grows.

Leaders who make LEAD a continuous priority build a resilient, adaptable, and high-performing team that is prepared to navigate change, overcome challenges, and achieve long-term success.

# Chapter 13:

# Evaluating the Impact of LEAD on Team Performance

## *Introduction*

Implementing the **LEAD** framework—**Listening, Empathy, Accountability,** and **Decisiveness**—offers a pathway to stronger, more resilient teams. However, to truly understand the effectiveness of LEAD, leaders must evaluate its impact on team performance. This evaluation process involves measuring specific outcomes, gathering feedback, and analyzing changes over time to determine the framework's strengths and areas for improvement.

This chapter will explore key performance indicators (KPIs), assessment tools, and strategies for measuring the impact of LEAD practices on team dynamics and organizational goals. By regularly evaluating LEAD, leaders can make data-driven adjustments that sustain high performance and support continuous growth.

## *1. Defining Key Performance Indicators (KPIs) for LEAD*

### *Why KPIs Matter for Evaluating LEAD*

Key Performance Indicators (KPIs) provide measurable metrics that reflect the impact of LEAD principles on team outcomes.

Defining clear KPIs linked to **Listening, Empathy, Accountability,** and **Decisiveness** allows leaders to assess how well these principles are embedded in the team and their effect on productivity, engagement, and cohesion.

### *Examples of LEAD-Related KPIs*

1. **KPIs for Listening**

   - **Employee Engagement Score**: Regular engagement surveys can reflect how well team members feel listened to and valued.

   - **Customer Satisfaction**: For customer-facing teams, measuring satisfaction scores can show the impact of listening to customer needs.

2. **KPIs for Empathy**

   - **Employee Retention Rate**: High empathy among leaders often correlates with improved retention, as team members feel supported and understood.

   - **Team Cohesion Score**: Use survey questions to gauge the level of trust and mutual support within the team.

3. **KPIs for Accountability**

   - **Goal Completion Rate**: Track the percentage of individual and team goals completed on time, as accountability influences follow-through.

- o **Quality of Work**: Monitor error rates or rework rates to evaluate how accountability impacts work quality.

4. **KPIs for Decisiveness**

- o **Decision-Making Efficiency**: Track the average time taken to make key decisions, reflecting the team's ability to act quickly.

- o **Project Timeliness**: Measure the rate of on-time project completion, as decisiveness often impacts deadlines.

## *Real-World Example: KPI Tracking*

A software development team set KPIs that included engagement scores, project completion times, and error rates. By tracking these KPIs, the team observed a 15% increase in on-time project delivery and a reduction in error rates, which they attributed to enhanced accountability and decisiveness from LEAD practices.

# *2. Conducting LEAD Impact Surveys*

## *The Role of Surveys in Evaluating LEAD*

Surveys provide direct feedback from team members about their experience with LEAD principles and their impact on team culture. Conducting regular LEAD impact surveys helps leaders gauge how well **Listening, Empathy, Accountability,** and **Decisiveness** are integrated into daily practices and highlights areas for improvement.

## *Tips for Conducting Effective LEAD Surveys*

1. **Use Clear, Specific Questions**

   o   Design questions that focus on each LEAD principle. For example, "Do you feel that team leaders actively listen to your concerns?" or "Are you encouraged to make decisive choices in your role?"

2. **Include Open-Ended Questions**

   o   Give respondents the chance to provide detailed feedback with questions like, "What specific LEAD practices have positively impacted your work experience?" This qualitative feedback provides deeper insights into team dynamics.

3. **Track Changes Over Time**

   o   Conduct surveys at regular intervals (e.g., quarterly or biannually) to assess response changes. Tracking trends over time shows how LEAD practices evolve and how they affect team morale, engagement, and productivity.

## *Real-World Example: LEAD Surveys*

A financial services firm conducted biannual LEAD impact surveys to assess team members' perceptions of listening and accountability practices. The survey results helped the firm identify that empathy practices needed improvement, prompting additional training for leaders. Subsequent surveys showed a 20% increase in team satisfaction.

# 3. Using 360-degree Feedback for Comprehensive Insights

## How 360-Degree Feedback Supports LEAD Evaluation

360-degree feedback involves gathering input from multiple sources, including peers, supervisors, and direct reports. This feedback method provides a well-rounded view of how effectively leaders and team members are applying LEAD principles. 360-degree feedback is particularly valuable in identifying areas for improvement and recognizing strengths.

## Techniques for LEAD-Centered 360-Degree Feedback

1. **Ask LEAD-Specific Questions**

   o Develop questions tailored to each LEAD principle. For example, "Does this team member demonstrate empathy?" or "How effectively does this person take accountability for their actions?"

2. **Analyze Trends Across Respondent Groups**

   o Compare feedback from different respondent groups to identify patterns. For example, if direct reports consistently rate a leader's empathy low, this may indicate a need for further empathy training.

3. **Provide Actionable Development Plans**

   o Use feedback results to create individualized development plans that address specific areas for improvement, ensuring that leaders continue to grow in LEAD competencies.

### *Real-World Example: 360-Degree Feedback*

A manufacturing firm implemented 360-degree feedback to evaluate accountability and decisiveness across production teams. The feedback revealed that while accountability was high, decisiveness needed improvement. Managers were trained in decision-making skills, leading to faster problem-solving on the production floor.

# 4. Conducting Case Studies of LEAD in Action

### *The Benefits of Case Studies for In-Depth Evaluation*

Case studies provide a qualitative way to examine specific examples of how LEAD principles have positively impacted the team. By analyzing real-life applications of **Listening, Empathy, Accountability,** and **Decisiveness**, leaders can gain insights into best practices and challenges, allowing them to refine their approach to LEAD.

### *Steps for Creating LEAD Case Studies*

1. **Identify LEAD Success Stories**

   o Look for examples where LEAD principles led to notable outcomes, such as resolving a conflict through empathy or improving project timelines through decisiveness.

2. **Gather Data and Testimonials**

   o Interview team members involved in the case to gather their perspectives on what worked well and any challenges they encountered. Data and testimonials bring the case study to life and offer concrete insights.

3. **Analyze Outcomes and Lessons Learned**

   o Evaluate the case study to identify factors that contributed to success and areas for potential improvement. Summarize lessons learned so that other teams can benefit from these insights.

## *Real-World Example: Case Study*

A university's administrative department conducted a case study on how accountability practices helped streamline student services. Through interviews and data analysis, they found that increased accountability led to a 30% reduction in service response times, demonstrating the value of LEAD in improving operational efficiency.

# 5. *Tracking Longitudinal Data for LEAD's Long-Term Impact*

## *The Importance of Longitudinal Data in Evaluating LEAD*

Longitudinal data provides a comprehensive view of LEAD's impact over time, showing how the integration of **Listening, Empathy, Accountability,** and **Decisiveness** affects the team's performance and resilience. Tracking data longitudinally allows leaders to observe trends, assess improvements, and make evidence-based adjustments to their LEAD strategy.

## *Steps for Tracking Longitudinal LEAD Data*

1. **Identify Key Metrics to Track Over Time**

   o Choose metrics that reflect the impact of LEAD principles, such as employee satisfaction scores, turnover rates, and project success rates. Tracking these metrics over time shows how LEAD practices influence the team's stability and growth.

2. **Create Regular LEAD Performance Reports**

   o Generate reports that analyze these metrics quarterly or annually, highlighting changes and patterns. Regular reports help leaders assess the sustainability of LEAD practices and make adjustments when needed.

3. **Use Longitudinal Data for Continuous Improvement**

   o Use the insights from longitudinal data to refine LEAD practices. For example, if a metric like employee satisfaction begins to decline, leaders can focus on strengthening listening or empathy practices to address underlying issues.

### *Real-World Example: Longitudinal Data Tracking*

A tech start-up tracked employee engagement and productivity rates over two years to evaluate LEAD's long-term impact. The data showed a steady increase in engagement scores and productivity, reinforcing that LEAD practices had a lasting positive effect on team dynamics.

# *Conclusion: LEAD as a Measurable and Impactful Leadership Framework*

Evaluating the impact of the **LEAD** framework—**Listening, Empathy, Accountability,** and **Decisiveness**—through KPIs, surveys, 360-degree feedback, case studies, and longitudinal data allows leaders to gain a comprehensive view of LEAD's effectiveness. Regular evaluation provides valuable insights into how these principles influence team performance, allowing leaders to adjust and refine their approach over time.

Leaders who commit to evaluating LEAD's impact strengthen their teams and demonstrate a commitment to adaptive, data-informed leadership.

**By continuously measuring and enhancing LEAD practices,** leaders can ensure that **Listening, Empathy, Accountability,** and **Decisiveness** remain central to the team's culture and performance. This ongoing evaluation builds a resilient team prepared to adapt, improve, and sustain high performance over time.

# *Chapter 14:*

# Conclusion – Becoming an Adaptive Leader for the Modern Workforce

## *Introduction*

In today's complex and evolving work environment, adaptive leadership is essential for navigating change, fostering resilience, and driving team success. The **LEAD** framework—**Listening, Empathy, Accountability,** and **Decisiveness**—offers a comprehensive, people-centered approach that empowers leaders to meet the demands of a modern workforce.

Throughout this book, we've explored how LEAD principles can transform team dynamics, encourage growth, and address challenges. From establishing trust through listening and empathy to promoting responsibility through accountability and decisiveness, the LEAD framework supports leaders in building cohesive, high-performing teams. In this concluding chapter, we'll review the key takeaways from each principle and provide actionable insights for leaders committed to creating sustainable, adaptable, and inspiring team cultures.

# *The Journey of LEAD: Key Takeaways*

### 1. Listening: The Foundation of Connection and Trust

- o Effective listening enables leaders to connect with their team, understand individual needs, and build a foundation of trust. Leaders who prioritize listening create an environment where team members feel heard and valued, which strengthens communication and engagement.

### 2. Empathy: Creating a Supportive and Inclusive Culture

- o Empathy allows leaders to understand and respond to team members' challenges, fostering a sense of belonging and mutual respect. Empathetic leaders build supportive environments where individuals feel valued, reducing burnout and increasing team resilience.

### 3. Accountability: Building Reliability and Integrity

- o Accountability reinforces commitment to personal and team goals, fostering a culture of trust and integrity. Leaders who emphasize accountability set clear expectations and celebrate responsibility, empowering team members to take ownership of their roles and contribute meaningfully.

4. **Decisiveness: Providing Clarity and Confidence**

   o Decisiveness supports effective decision-making, promoting clarity, direction, and momentum. Leaders who act decisively empower their teams to take initiative, adapt quickly, and maintain focus, even in challenging situations.

Together, these principles enable leaders to create a team culture that is adaptable, cohesive, and purpose-driven. By making LEAD an integral part of their leadership approach, leaders cultivate an environment that can navigate change, seize opportunities, and achieve sustained success.

# *Final Insights for Implementing LEAD in the Modern Workforce*

1. **Embrace Continuous Learning and Adaptability**

   o Leadership is not static; it requires ongoing growth and a willingness to evolve. Leaders committed to the LEAD framework must continually refine their approach based on team feedback, emerging challenges, and evolving organizational goals. Embracing continuous learning ensures that LEAD practices remain relevant and responsive to team needs.

2.  **Prioritize People-Centered Leadership**

    o   The LEAD framework emphasizes a people-centered approach, recognizing that team members are the core of any organization. Leaders who focus on building strong relationships, supporting well-being, and fostering collaboration create a motivated and resilient team capable of achieving remarkable results.

3.  **Align LEAD with Organizational Goals and Vision**

    o   Aligning LEAD principles with broader organizational goals reinforces their importance and ensures that all efforts support a unified mission. Leaders who connect LEAD practices with the organization's vision cultivate a culture where adaptability and innovation are celebrated as essential elements of success.

4.  **Lead by Example and Model LEAD Values**

    o   To sustain LEAD principles, leaders must model **Listening, Empathy, Accountability,** and **Decisiveness** in their own actions. When leaders demonstrate these values, they set the standard for the team, inspiring team members to adopt LEAD principles in their own roles and interactions.

### 5. Foster a Growth Mindset Across the Team

- ○ Encourage a growth mindset by promoting the idea that challenges are opportunities for learning and development. Leaders who foster a growth mindset help team members embrace change with optimism and resilience, creating a culture where improvement and adaptability are valued.

# *A Call to Action for Future Leaders*

As you move forward in your leadership journey, remember that the LEAD framework is not just a set of practices but a commitment to creating meaningful, lasting impact. The modern workforce requires agile, empathetic, and purposeful leaders, and LEAD provides a roadmap to achieve these qualities.

Whether you're leading a small team or overseeing a large department, applying **Listening, Empathy, Accountability,** and **Decisiveness** will help you build a culture of trust, collaboration, and high performance. By embracing and integrating these values into your daily practices, you'll inspire your team to achieve new heights, foster a lasting sense of unity, and become a beacon of adaptive leadership in today's world.

# *In Summary: The Power of LEAD in Modern Leadership*

The LEAD framework offers leaders a timeless approach to building adaptable, resilient, and united teams. By prioritizing **Listening, Empathy, Accountability,** and **Decisiveness**, you empower your team to work collaboratively, grow continuously, and face challenges with confidence. LEAD is more than a framework— it's a foundation for meaningful leadership that creates positive change, encourages growth, and drives sustainable success.

As you continue to apply LEAD in your leadership journey, remember that each interaction, decision, and action has the potential to shape team culture and inspire future leaders. Embrace LEAD with intention and commitment, and you'll contribute to a workforce that values adaptability, respect, and purpose.

Thank you for embarking on this journey with LEAD. May this framework guide you as you lead with strength, vision, and integrity in the ever-evolving world of work.

With **Chapter 15** complete, we've concluded the journey through the LEAD framework. This final chapter emphasized the importance of adaptive leadership in the modern workplace and offered actionable insights for integrating LEAD into long-term leadership practices. The LEAD principles of **Listening, Empathy, Accountability,** and **Decisiveness** are powerful tools that, when applied thoughtfully, create resilient, engaged, and high-performing teams. Thank you for following along on this journey to adaptive leadership!

# *Closing Summary*

The journey through *LEAD: Empowering Adaptive Leadership* has taken us from the foundational principles of Listening, Empathy, Accountability, and Decisiveness to the advanced applications of these values across various organizational challenges. In each chapter, we have explored how adaptive leaders can cultivate teams that are resilient, collaborative, and aligned with a shared purpose.

Through the LEAD framework, you've gained tools and strategies for building trust, fostering cohesion, and addressing conflicts constructively. You've learned how to adapt your leadership style to meet your team's evolving needs and how to sustain LEAD principles over time, embedding them into the culture for long-term impact. The real-world examples, case studies, and actionable exercises throughout this book provide a practical foundation to help you implement these principles.

In a rapidly changing world, LEAD equips leaders with the agility, insight, and interpersonal awareness needed to navigate the complexities of today's workplace. By committing to LEAD, you're not just adopting a leadership model—you're committing to creating a positive, empowering environment where both leaders and team members can thrive.

As you move forward, remember that leadership is an evolving journey. Continue to listen deeply, lead with empathy, uphold accountability, and make clear, confident decisions. By integrating these values into your daily interactions, you'll drive performance and inspire those around you to bring their best selves to work each day.

Thank you for embarking on this journey with LEAD. May these principles guide you as you shape a high-performing, adaptable team prepared to meet the challenges and seize the opportunities of tomorrow's workplace.